Linda Chapman lives in Leicestershire with her husband, daughter and two Bernese mountain dogs. She used to be a stage manager in the theatre. When she is not writing she spends her time horse riding, putting on plays and teaching drama.

BRIGHT lights

Linda Chapman

PUFFIN BOOKS

PUFFIN BOOKS

Published by the Penguin Group
Penguin Books Ltd, 80 Strand, London WC2R 0RL, England
Penguin Putnam Inc., 375 Hudson Street, New York, New York 10014, USA
Penguin Books Australia Ltd, 250 Camberwell Road, Camberwell, Victoria 3124, Australia
Penguin Books Canada Ltd, 10 Alcorn Avenue, Toronto, Ontario, Canada M4V 3B2
Penguin Books India (P) Ltd, 11 Community Centre, Panchsheel Park, New Delhi – 110 017, India
Penguin Books (NZ) Ltd, Cnr Rosedale and Airborne Roads, Albany, Auckland, New Zealand
Penguin Books (South Africa) (Pty) Ltd, 24 Sturdee Avenue, Rosebank 2196, South Africa

Penguin Books Ltd, Registered Offices: 80 Strand, London WC2R 0RL, England

www.penguin.com

First published 2003
3

Set in Monotype Perpetua
Typeset by Rowland Phototypesetting Ltd, Bury St Edmunds, Suffolk
Made and printed in England by Clays Ltd, St Ives plc

British Library Cataloguing in Publication Data
A CIP catalogue record for this book is available from the British Library

ISBN 0–141–31617–9

To Peter — for letting me follow my dreams

A huge thank you to all the Bright Stars in Wymeswold, especially Nicole and Hope Dawkins, Laura and Sophie Tebbutt and Michelle Emmet for giving me so many ideas about friends, sleepovers and brothers and sisters (you love them really!). Thanks too, must go to Alison at Carlton Junior TV Workshop and to Grace, Laura, Siobhan, Jack and Nicholas who gave up their time to talk to me about what it is like to be a young TV/film actor. Special thanks to Sarah Hughes at Puffin and Philippa Milnes-Smith at LAW for all their wonderful input and ideas and to Caroline Piggott for her never-ending support and friendship. Lastly, the biggest thank you of all must go to Peter and Iola — for everything.

Chapter One

'He is dead,' I whispered.

I knelt beside the body of the great lion. The only sound in the packed room was the occasional weeping of an overcome parent.

Suddenly a voice called across the school lunch hall. 'Lucy!'

'Yes!' I answered, jerking out of my daydream and almost knocking my plate of sausage and chips on to the floor. 'Me! I'm Lucy!'

The year-five girl looked at me in surprise before walking off with her friend, Lucy Roberts, who had been sitting at the next-door table.

My two best friends, Ally Swannick and Harriet Chase, stared at me as if I was an escaped lunatic.

'OK, Sophie,' Ally said slowly. 'Have you finally gone *totally* mad?'

Talk about embarrassing! Nearly everyone in the lunch hall was looking at me now. I sank down in my chair, my cheeks as red as the reddest thing you can imagine. It's not that I mind being the centre of attention, it's just that I'd rather not be making a complete idiot of myself at the time!

As usual, Harriet was the first to figure out what was going on in my mind. 'I get it!' she said suddenly. 'You were thinking about the play, weren't you? You were thinking about being Lucy?'

I risked a look round the room. Everyone had lost interest in me and the conversations were starting up again. I nodded. 'I could just see the stage in my mind,' I explained. 'I was imagining the audience and what it would be like to be Lucy, so when I heard someone say, "Lucy!" I just said, "Yes."'

Ally shook her head. 'Sometimes, Sophie, you are seriously weird!'

Rapidly recovering from my embarrassment, I sat up in my chair and grinned at her. 'You can talk!' Before she could come back with a reply, I let out a longing sigh. 'I just want to be Lucy so much.'

'You will be,' Harriet said, her hazel eyes confident. 'I bet you will.'

You have no idea how much I wanted to believe her. Getting the part of Lucy was the only thing I'd been able to think about all last week – ever since our teacher, Miss Carter, had told us that the school play for the summer was going to be *The Lion, the Witch and the Wardrobe*. It's one of my all-time favourite books. It's about four children who go through a wardrobe and end up in a magic land called Narnia. Lucy's the youngest and the bravest. I was desperate to be her. And now there wasn't long to wait. That very afternoon Miss Carter was going to give out the parts.

'I don't know what you're stressing about anyway, Soph,' Ally said, shrugging. 'You always get the main part whenever we do a play.'

'Ally's right,' Harriet agreed. 'There's no way Miss Carter would choose anyone else to be Lucy. You're easily the best at acting in the class.'

I shot them grateful looks. Ally and Harriet are the best friends ever. They might not be into acting themselves, but they understand how much it means to me. I'm not particularly brilliant at anything else – not like Harriet, who's nearly always top at everything – but I know I'm good at acting. When I leave school I want to go to drama college and become a famous actress, like Kate Winslet or Julia Roberts.

'I wonder what parts we'll get,' Harriet said to Ally as we stood up to clear away our plates.

'Dunno,' Ally said. 'I hope I don't have too many lines to learn though.'

She pushed her blonde hair back behind her ears. It used to be long, but last month she had it cut and now it curls under by her chin. She's really pretty, with big brown eyes and a wide smiley mouth. People always think she looks so sweet, but she loves playing jokes and she's got a real temper when she's angry.

Harriet, on the other hand, never argues with

anyone. She's very patient and quiet. People who don't know her well think she's serious, but she's actually really good fun. She's tall, with freckles and long browny-blonde hair that she usually ties back in a pony-tail. We've been friends for eight years – ever since we started at our village playgroup when we were three.

Ally's been our friend for two years. She started at our school in year four and was put on the same table as me in class. From the first day, when she handed out trick sweets to all the boys, she's always been really good fun. At first she and Harriet didn't get on – they both wanted to be my best friend. But after a bit they started horse-riding together and now they get on very well.

As for what I look like, well, I've got very thick dark-brown shoulder-length hair, big grey-blue eyes that seem to take up my whole face and a pointed chin. I'm also the smallest girl in year six. When I was younger, my older brother, Tom, used to tease me and say I was a pixie who'd been swapped at birth. Older brothers can be *so* annoying!

'Come on! Let's go outside,' Harriet said as we dumped our plates and trays.

We headed for our favourite place – the wall by the climbing frame. There was the usual chaos in the playground – the little ones running round, the year-five and year-six boys playing football and showing off on the climbing frame, groups of girls talking or doing gymnastics on the grass.

'Uh-oh,' Harriet said suddenly under her breath. 'Look who's heading this way.'

Justine Wilcox was walking towards us, holding hands with Kevin Donaghue. Justine's our *least* favourite girl in the class. Flicking her long blonde hair, she smiled smugly as she walked by. It was as if she thought we should all be really jealous of her for having Kevin as her boyfriend. I mean, pur-lease! I'd never go out with Kevin. In fact, I wouldn't go out with *any* of the boys in our class. They are *so* immature. If I was going to have a boyfriend, I'd want to go out with someone really nice like Dan, who is the boyfriend of my sister, Jessica. For a moment I imagined walking round the school playground with Dan – tall, dark and handsome, a bit like Freddie Prinz Junior, when Freddie Prinz Junior is looking normal, of course, not how he looks in *Scooby Doo*.

'Sophie! Earth to Sophie!'

I came out of my daydream with a jump as Ally waved her hand in front of my face. She grinned at me. 'What was that goofy look at Kevin for?'

I realized I must have been staring dreamily at Kevin as he walked past. 'Nothing,' I said quickly.

Ally nudged Harriet. 'Sophie fancies Kevin.'

'I do not!' I exclaimed.

'Do so,' Ally said triumphantly. 'You should have seen the way you were looking at him, you –'

'I was thinking about Dan!' I interrupted.

'Ohhhhh.' Ally nodded in sudden understanding. She and Harriet thought Dan was mega-fit too.

'Why can't we have boyfriends like him?' sighed Harriet.

'Umm – because we're not fourteen and we don't look like Jess,' I suggested. My sister is seriously pretty, with long wavy hair and a figure that goes in and out in all the right places.

'You are *so* lucky having Jessica as a sister,' Harriet said.

I nodded. I know I am. Lots of people I know don't get on with their sisters – Harriet and her older sister, Emily, fight all the time. But Jess is really cool. We argue sometimes, of course, but we almost never really fall out in a major way. It's almost like having another best friend.

The school bell rang. All thoughts of Jessica and Dan left my head. 'It's the bell!' I gasped.

Ally grinned. 'Yes, Sophie – it rings every day about this time.'

'But that means . . . that means we're going to find out the parts for the play!' My heart raced.

'And you're going to get the part of Lucy,' Ally said, jumping off the wall and pulling me with her. 'Come on!'

The three of us headed towards the entrance. As we reached it, Justine Wilcox pushed in front of us. She had left Kevin and was with her friends, Saskia and Julie.

They hardly even glanced at us. They think they're just so cool. Saskia and Julie didn't used to be too bad, but then Justine started in our class at the beginning of the year and since they became friends with her all they ever do is talk about make-up and clothes – I mean, how sad!

As we waited in the queue to go inside, Justine fluffed up her hair. 'I can't wait to hear who's got which part in the play,' she said to Julie and Saskia. 'I told Miss Carter yesterday that I really wanted to be Lucy. I hope she lets me.'

I grabbed Harriet's arm. 'Did you hear what Justine just said?' I hissed as we started walking inside.

'Don't worry,' Harriet said reassuringly. 'She won't get the part.'

'But she's quite good at acting and you know Miss Carter likes her.' That's the trouble with teachers: they are so easily fooled into thinking someone's sweet and nice when they don't see them out of lessons.

Harriet squeezed my hand. 'You're way better than Justine, Soph. You'll be Lucy. I know you will.'

I hoped she was right.

Miss Carter was waiting for us in the classroom. On her desk was a large pile of scripts. I swallowed. This was it: the moment I'd been waiting for.

'OK, everyone, sit down,' Miss Carter instructed.

It seemed to take forever for everyone to settle in their chairs but at last there was quiet.

'Well,' Miss Carter said, smiling round at us, 'I won't keep you in suspense any longer. I'm sure you're all keen to find out what part you're going to play, so here we go. The part of Lucy will be played by . . .'

I caught my breath and crossed every single finger and toe.

'. . . Justine Wilcox,' Miss Carter announced.

Chapter Two

'Yessss!' I heard Justine Wilcox whisper in triumph.

'No!' I gasped in horror.

Everyone swung round in their seats to stare at me. My face blushed bright red.

'Sophie?' Miss Carter questioned. 'Are you all right?'

I wanted to die. Why had I spoken out loud? 'I'm fine, Miss,' I mumbled, looking down at my desk. From the far side of the room I could sense Justine Wilcox's ice-blue eyes looking at me and I knew, just knew, that there'd be a smirk on her face.

Miss Carter cleared her throat and continued. 'The part of Susan will be played by Sunita, the White Witch by Charlotte, the . . .'

I'm not Lucy. I'm not Lucy. The words went round and round in my head. It felt as if I was in a nightmare. There had to be some mistake. I had to be Lucy.

Suddenly a thought crept into my shocked brain. *If I'm not Lucy, who am I going to be?*

'And now on to the smaller parts,' Miss Carter said. 'Ally, you're going to be a hedgehog. Max, you're going

to be a faun. Harriet, you will be a fox, and Sophie –'
I looked up – 'you will be the chief squirrel.'

I felt a stab of disbelief. *Chief squirrel!* After all my
dreams of playing Lucy! I stared at Miss Carter. How
could she do this to me?

But Miss Carter was already looking away at the
next person on her list. My head swam. A squirrel! I was
a measly squirrel!

As Miss Carter finished, she handed out the scripts.
'I'll give them to you now so you can read them through
and start learning your lines, but we won't start rehearsing properly until after the SATs in a few weeks' time.'

I took the script I was handed and looked through
the pages. The chief squirrel had four lines. Four lines! I
shut the script in disgust.

'Now, can you put your scripts away in your drawers
and get out your design projects please?' Miss Carter said.

There was a scraping of chairs and a buzz of excited
chatter. I saw Ally and Harriet heading towards me, but
before they could reach me Miss Carter stopped in front
of me.

'I hope you're not too upset at having a smaller part
this year, Sophie,' she said. 'You've had a main part the
last two years and I thought it might be nice to let
someone else have a go. You don't mind, do you?'

Mind? Of course I mind! I felt like shouting. But I didn't.
I just shook my head and forced a smile, as if being a
squirrel instead of Lucy was just fine by me.

'Good,' Miss Carter said, smiling at me. 'I knew you'd understand.'

'It's so unfair,' I said for about the hundredth time as I walked home through the village with Ally and Harriet. They were both coming back to mine for tea. 'I can't believe Justine is going to be Lucy and not me.'

'You'd have been loads better than her,' Harriet said loyally.

Ally's brown eyes flashed with indignation. 'I think it was really horrid of Miss Carter. How could she be so mean?'

Harriet frowned. 'Ally! You know Miss Carter wasn't trying to be mean. You heard what she said – she was only trying to let other people have the main parts for a change.'

Harriet's my best friend ever, but sometimes I wish she wasn't always so nice about everyone!

'Well, I think Miss Carter was being mean,' Ally said. She linked arms with me. 'Horrible Miss Carter,' she said, looking at me for agreement.

The trouble was, although I wanted to agree with Ally, deep down I knew Harriet was right. I sighed. 'Miss Carter's not horrible. I guess she wasn't trying to be nasty to me.'

'And anyway, look on the bright side, Soph,' Harriet said optimistically. 'You won't have all those lines to learn now.'

A deep wave of gloom engulfed me. 'But I want lines to learn,' I protested. 'And now I'm not going to be in another play for ages.' Next year we would all be at Charles Hope secondary school and there you didn't get to do a play until you were in year nine – three whole years away! 'Oh, this is so unfair!' I burst out again at the thought.

We walked on in silence.

'Look, there's Tom,' Ally pointed out suddenly.

I looked up. My older brother was sitting on the church wall with some of his friends. He ignored me. He's fifteen and although we get on just fine at home, he usually acts like I don't exist when he's outside with his mates.

'How are the Blue Lemons?' Ally asked as we turned down the lane at the side of the church that led to my house.

I forced myself to think about something other than my disappointment. 'OK, I think.'

Tom had started a band called the Blue Lemons with his best friends, Nick and Raj, and Nick's cousin, Zak. They always seemed to be round at Nick's house, practising.

Suddenly I remembered some news I'd heard the night before. 'Tom said they're going to play at our school fair at the end of term. Nick's dad's a member of the PTA and he asked them.'

'That's brilliant!' Ally exclaimed, looking well

impressed. She's very into music. 'How come you didn't tell us sooner?'

I shrugged. 'It didn't seem important.'

'Not important!' Ally said, looking at me as if I was mad. 'But just think how cool it'll be – we'll know the band!'

Harriet and I exchanged glances and I could tell she was as excited by Tom's band playing as I was – in other words, not very. I mean, it would be quite fun, but it was just my brother and his mates.

Ally grinned. 'Just imagine how jealous Justine will be when she finds out your brother's in the band!'

Thinking about Justine, I remembered about the play and sighed heavily.

'Come on, Soph! Cheer up,' Ally said happily. 'You might not have got the part of Lucy, but Tom's playing at the school fair.'

Yeah, like that made me feel loads better – *not*!

We reached my house. It's an old cottage that's tucked away behind the church. There's a smart blue front door that leads on to the street, but no one ever uses that because it goes straight into the lounge. Instead we go through the gate at the side of house, up a paved area we call the yard and in through the back door.

As I opened the gate, Wilson and Baxter, our two black Labradors, came hurtling round from the back garden into the yard.

'Hi, boys,' I said, patting them as they bounced around us, whining in delight.

With their thick tails thwacking against our legs, we fought our way to the kitchen. Jessica was getting herself a drink from the fridge. Even wearing her boring school uniform – navy trousers and jumper – she managed to look like a model. Her long wavy hair was tied into a loose ponytail, with just a few strands escaping around her face. She turned as we came in. 'Hi there,' she said. 'Do you three want a drink?'

We all nodded. Jessica tossed us a can of Coke each. 'Did you get the part, then, Soph?'

'No,' I muttered, sitting down at the big pine table.

'Justine Wilcox got it,' Ally explained.

'Bummer,' Jess said, looking at me sympathetically.

I was about to nod when suddenly through the window I caught sight of Mum by the gate. She had several bags of groceries and was wearing a smart black trouser suit.

'Mum's home!' I said.

Leaping up, I grabbed Wilson while Jessica caught Baxter. Every evening we have the same routine. Baxter and Wilson seem to believe it's their doggy duty to cover smart clothes of any description in slobber and black hair – particularly Mum's work clothes.

'Thanks, you two!' Mum said gratefully as we held the dogs back while she came in. 'I'll pat you in a minute,' she promised the dogs. 'Just as soon as I've got changed.' She smiled at Ally and Harriet as she dumped the shopping bags on the floor. 'Hi, girls.'

Baxter and Wilson whined and desperately tried to get to Mum. Jessica and I quickly dragged them outside, their paws scrabbling on the old terracotta-tiled floor.

Mum sighed and sat down. 'What a day!' she said, as Jess patted the dogs and shut the door. 'Boring paperwork, taking obnoxious phone calls, being nice to rude people. Sometimes I really do wonder why I work in an office.'

'You do it for the money,' Jess said, putting her arms round Mum's neck. 'So you can buy us things – like those embroidered jeans I saw at Top Shop at the weekend.' She kissed Mum on the cheek. 'Only kidding. Cup of tea?' she asked, heading for the kettle.

Mum smiled gratefully and Jessica switched the kettle on. 'You should change your job if you really don't like it, Mum,' she said.

I nodded. 'Do something else.'

'It's a nice idea,' Mum said. 'But I'm not exactly qualificd to do anything else. Though it would be lovely to be in a job where I didn't have to look smart all the time.' She ruefully brushed the hairs off her trousers. 'Anyway, come on, Sophie. Tell me all. Did you get the part you wanted?'

I so wanted to be able to say yes. I swallowed and shook my head.

'Oh, well, never mind,' Mum said, shrugging as if it didn't matter.

I stared at her. 'Never mind!' I exclaimed.

'I mean, it's not like it's the end of the world, is it?' Mum continued lightly. 'Something else will come along.'

'No, it won't!' I cried, feeling totally betrayed by her lack of sympathy. 'Mum! I can't believe you think it doesn't matter. I've got nothing to look forward to now – not for ages. I . . . I . . .' I struggled to find words to tell her how awful I felt. 'I might just as well die!'

OK, so maybe that was a tiny bit extreme, but what did she expect? Telling me not to mind, as if all that had happened was that I'd had some tiny disappointment.

'Oh, well, if you want to die, you won't be interested in seeing this,' Mum said, pulling a newspaper cutting from her bag and holding it up casually.

'What is it?' I demanded.

'Just an article from the local paper saying that a film company is going to be filming near here in the summer and is looking for local children between eight and thirteen to be extras,' Mum said, her eyes twinkling. 'But of course, you're not interested – you want to die.' She started to fold up the cutting. 'So I suppose I might as well throw this away.'

'No! Don't!' I flew to her side. 'Let me see.'

Mum handed me the article with a smile.

I read:

STAR STRUCK!

Have you got a daughter between eight and thirteen years old who wants to be a film star? Well, read on! Griffin Film Production is going to be filming *A Little Princess* (based on the classic children's book of the same name by Frances Hodgson Burnett) in the East Midlands over the summer holidays and is looking for twenty lucky local girls to take on non-speaking roles in the film. Auditions are to be held on Saturday 1 May and Sunday 2 May in Nottingham. Anyone interested should phone Griffin Film Production on the number below.

'Can I audition?' I gasped.

Mum nodded.

I shoved the cutting into Ally's hand. 'Look, it's a film. We can all audition.'

Ally and Harriet glanced over the article together.

Harriet quickly shook her head. 'I don't think I will. There's going to be lots of pony days at the riding school in July and August. We get to look after a pony for the whole day. You groom it and muck it out and clean its tack. I don't want to miss that.'

Ally nodded. 'There's going to be a gymkhana and jumping competitions with rosettes. I really want to win a rosette.'

I stared at them. Were they on a different planet?

How *could* they turn down the chance to be in a film just because of a few pony days at their riding school?

'But this is a film!' I told them in disbelief. 'A proper film.'

Ally and Harriet just shrugged.

'I wish I was young enough to audition,' Jessica said, reading the cutting over Ally's shoulder. 'It sounds cool.'

It sounded more than just cool to me! Inside I was almost fainting with excitement.

I swung round to Mum. 'Will you ring?' I begged. 'Will you ring now?'

Mum nodded and stood up. 'All right. Pass me the number.'

I paced impatiently around the kitchen while Mum rang up and spoke to someone at the film company.

'I see . . . That sounds fine . . . Yes, she's eleven years old . . . Yes, we can make that time . . . OK . . . OK . . . I see . . .'

'Well?' I demanded the second Mum put the phone down. 'What did they say?'

'You've got an audition booked for two thirty on Saturday afternoon.'

'Yes!' I cried, my tummy doing a triple somersault in delight.

'They're going to send us a form to fill in with all your details,' Mum said, 'and we need to take in a photo of you. Don't go getting too excited though,' she warned me. 'The girl I spoke to said there are lots of people ringing up for auditions.' She took the cup of tea that Jessica had made her. 'Now, I'm going to get changed. Remember, it's your turn to feed the animals tonight, Sophie.'

I nodded distractedly as she and Jessica left the room. I could be in a film!

'Hello – is there anyone there?' Ally teased, waving a hand in front of my face.

'Uh . . . what?' I said, blinking.

Harriet plonked the dog bowls in front of me. 'Dogs. Feed,' she said.

I came down to earth with a bump. 'I wonder what I'll have to do at the audition?' I said as I fetched a tin-opener to open the can of dog food Ally was taking out from the cupboard under the sink.

'Maybe the form they're sending will say,' Harriet suggested, getting out the rabbit food. She and Ally knew the pet-feeding routine at my house very well.

'I'll have to read the book again,' I said, trying to remember the story of *A Little Princess*. I opened the tin and started forking meat into the bowls. 'I read it ages ago. I can't remember what happens.'

'It's about a girl called Sara who gets sent to a boarding school,' Harriet said. She loves books and has hundreds at her house. 'She starts off really rich and everyone likes her and treats her like a princess, but then her father dies and she's really poor. She becomes a maid at the school and has to live in the attic. Most of her old friends won't speak to her and the headmistress is really horrid to her. She's best friends with the other maid, Becky, and they make up all these stories and then she gets rescued and it all ends OK.'

'Yeah, that's it,' I said, remembering. 'The man who moves in next door was her father's business partner. He's in England looking for her because it turns out that her father did leave her lots of money after all.'

'So she ends up rich again,' Harriet said. 'And she lives with the man next door and never has to go to the horrid boarding school again. And Becky the maid goes to live with them too.'

'It sounds a bit old-fashioned,' Ally said, frowning as she refilled the dogs' water bowl.

'Well, it is set in the old days,' Harriet explained. 'Before cars and things.'

The second I opened the door, Baxter and Wilson charged at me like two Labrador-shaped torpedoes. As soon as I put the bowls down, they started gobbling the food as if they hadn't eaten for weeks. Labradors have to be the greediest dogs in the world!

'Rabbits and guinea pigs now?' Ally said.

I nodded. We have three rabbits and two guinea pigs, all of whom we'd rescued. Mum can never say no when an animal needs a home.

We'd just finished feeding them and started putting some fresh hay in their hutches when Tom appeared.

'Guess what?' I said, hurrying down the yard to meet him. 'I'm auditioning to be in a film!'

Tom stopped. 'A film?' he said in surprise. 'What film?'

'It's called *A Little Princess*.'

'Oh, right,' Tom said. He paused for a moment and then shrugged. 'Cool.' He headed for the house.

I followed him. 'I'd be filming in the summer holidays. Wouldn't it be brilliant if I got in? Just imagine, I'd be in a film – a real film!'

'Sounds great, Soph.' Tom took two packets of crisps from the cupboard. 'Anyway, I'm going on the computer. See ya.' He headed into the lounge without a backward glance.

I stared after him. Could he be any more unexcited? Brothers! Shaking my head, I went out to join the others.

✦

Chapter Three

'It is *so* not fair,' I said, sitting on Jessica's bed four days later as she got ready to go out with Dan. 'I can't believe Mum won't let me have some photos done.'

'Mmm?' Jessica said absent-mindedly as she twisted her hair up with one hand and looked at herself in the mirror. She tilted her head to one side. 'What do you think? Up or down?'

'Jess!' I exclaimed. 'You're not listening.'

She turned to look at me. 'Yes, I am. You're moaning because Mum won't let you go and have a professional photo taken for this audition.'

'I'm not moaning,' I protested. 'I'm just saying it's really unfair.'

'I don't get why you're making such a big deal about it,' Jess said, turning back to the mirror. 'Mum said they just want a snapshot so they can remember what you look like after the audition. It doesn't matter if it's a brilliant picture or not.'

I sighed. OK, she was right, but it just *was* a big deal. At least it had been ever since I'd heard at school that day that Justine Wilcox was going to be auditioning too and that her mum was taking her to a professional photographer in Nottingham to have a photo done.

'Jessica!' Dad called up the stairs. 'Dan's here!'

Jessica jumped up. 'Help! I'm not ready!'

Leaving her to finish getting all glammed up, I went downstairs.

Dan was in the kitchen. 'Hi, Soph.' He smiled at me teasingly. 'I hear you're going to be a film star, then?'

'Well, I'm going for an audition,' I replied.

'Tomorrow afternoon, isn't it?' Dan said, nodding. 'Jess told me. Good luck.'

'Thanks,' I said, grinning at him. Dan's just so nice. Much nicer than most of the boys Jessica's been out with.

Just then Jessica came into the kitchen. She had left her hair down and it fell over her shoulders in shining dark waves. She was wearing a sky-blue top that matched her eyes and a long cream skirt. 'Hi there,' she greeted him.

He smiled and walked towards her. I could tell they were going to kiss.

'Er . . . see you later,' I said hastily.

I hurried out of the room. Yuck! Watching my sister snogging is *not* my idea of fun!

'Next group please,' the woman at the auditions said. She looked about twenty-five and was holding a clipboard. Her blonde hair was tied in two plaits.

I shifted on my hard plastic chair as five girls stood up and left the bare room. It was my turn next and my stomach suddenly seemed full of fluttering butterflies – not the small white ones we get in our garden in the summer but gigantic Amazonian butterflies like the ones Miss Carter showed us last term in a video about rainforests.

Across the room, I could hear the drone of Justine Wilcox's voice as she talked loudly to the girl next to her about how she'd got the lead part in her school play. 'Yeah, I'm Lucy,' she was saying. 'Our teacher said she thought I'd be just perfect for the part . . .'

I tried not to listen. I felt sick. I wanted to go to the toilet.

Mum squeezed my hand. 'It'll be OK.'

I gulped. I wished I could believe her.

Five minutes later, the door opened again and pony-tail girl came in. 'Next group please.'

I stood up, my knees wobbling as if they had turned to rubber.

'Good luck,' Mum said.

I swallowed. 'Thanks.'

'This way,' the girl said, holding the door open. 'If you come with me I'll tell you what you've got to do.'

She led us into another room a little further down the corridor. There were chairs around the outside and a clear space in the middle. 'I'm Cathy,' she said, shutting the door. 'I'm the third assistant director on the film. Steve Hanson will be auditioning you. He's the first assistant director. 'What he wants you to do is to prepare a short play showing someone's first day at a new school. You've got ten minutes to prepare something and then I'll come and fetch you.'

She left the room. We all stared at each other.

'We've got to do what?' one of the other girls said.

'A play,' I said.

My mind was already starting to work. A play. That was OK. I could do plays.

'We've just got to make it up!' Justine said. 'I thought we'd be reading some lines or something.'

'Me too,' one of the other girls said, looking panicked. 'I can't make up a play.'

'It's all right,' I said quickly, feeling my nerves start to subside. 'I think I've got an idea.'

OK, so maybe it wasn't brilliant, but my play was definitely all right. It was about a girl who was going to a new school and was really worried about what it would be like. In scene one she was talking to her mum about how worried she was, then in scene two she went to school and was very nervous, but in scene three she made friends. I made sure that everyone had lines to say and luckily, because no one else had any ideas, they didn't argue about what we did but just got on and practised, so by the time it was our turn to go in we had run through it three times and all knew what we were doing.

I was playing the girl who was new at school and I made sure that I spoke loudly, so that Steve could hear, and whenever anyone looked like they had forgotten what happened next I quickly said something to cover up. Justine was my mum and one of the people who became my friends. She was actually really good. She didn't forget anything and she didn't giggle or look embarrassed.

'Excellent!' Steve said, clapping at the end.

He was about thirty, with spiky blond hair. He was wearing combat trousers and a white T-shirt and didn't look nearly as scary as I'd been imagining a film director would look.

'That was great, girls. Now, come over here and tell me a little about yourselves.'

We went to the table he was sitting behind.

'We'll start with you,' he said, pointing to a girl called Beth who had spoken really quietly when we did the play.

'Er . . . um,' she stammered, looking like a startled rabbit caught in a car's headlamps.

'You're Beth, aren't you?' Steve said, looking down at our application forms and photos on his desk. 'Tell me what you like doing, Beth?'

'Er . . .' Beth looked like her mind had gone totally blank. 'I like . . . I like . . . playing tennis,' she gulped.

Steve smiled at her. 'Great,' he said kindly, then he moved on. 'And you?' he said, looking at me. 'Sophie, isn't it?'

I smiled and nodded. Now I had done the play, my nerves had gone completely.

'So, what do you like doing, Sophie?' Steve asked.

'Acting,' I answered, trying to sound bright and confident. There was no way I wanted to come across all shy like Beth. 'I mean, I like other things as well,' I told him. 'I love animals – we've got two dogs, three rabbits and two guinea pigs at home, and I like looking after them – but I like acting best.'

Steve nodded encouragingly. 'Have you done much acting?'

'Just school stuff. I was Dorothy when we did *The Wizard of Oz* last year.' Something told me I should keep talking for as long as I could and so I plunged on. 'This year I really wanted to be Lucy – we're doing *The Lion, the Witch and the Wardrobe*,' I explained. 'But I didn't get the part because my teacher said she wanted to let someone else have a go at having the main part. I was really upset, particularly when I heard what part I had got.'

'And what was that?' Steve asked.

I grinned. 'Chief squirrel. A really important part – *not*!'

To my delight, Steve laughed. He looked down at my notes. 'How old are you, Sophie?'

'Eleven,' I replied.

Steve nodded and I saw him scribble something on his notes. My heart leapt with excitement. He hadn't done that when Beth had spoken. Steve talked to the other girls. They were all quite shy – apart from Justine. She, of course, doesn't know the meaning of the word. She spoke loudly and smiled and twirled her hair. She told him about being Lucy, but she didn't make him laugh like I had. However, I saw him scribble something on her sheet as she finished speaking, just like he had on mine.

'Well, that's great for now,' he said. 'Let's take you back to your parents.'

He walked to the door. We all followed him back to the waiting room. 'Mrs Tennison?' Steve said. 'And Mrs Wilcox?'

My mum and Justine's mum exchanged surprised glances.

'Yes?' they both said, standing up.

'If I could just have a quick word with you and the girls outside,' Steve said.

For one moment I forgot how much Justine and I didn't get on. We stared at each other, the same feelings of hope and excitement leaping into our eyes.

'Sophie and Justine did very well,' Steve said to Mum and Mrs Wilcox when we left the waiting room. 'And what I'd like to discuss is the possibility of them auditioning for small speaking roles in the film. The main child parts are going to be played by experienced child actors, but we are hoping to cast some of the

28

smaller speaking roles from among the local children we've been seeing this weekend. It would only be to speak a line or two, but if Justine and Sophie are interested then they'll need to attend a further audition next week.'

I looked at Mum. 'Can I?' I gasped.

'I don't see why not,' she said.

'Justine's a super little actress. She'd be perfect for a speaking part,' Mrs Wilcox put in.

'Well, like I say, they'll both need to audition again,' Steve said. 'I'll put their names down on the list and contact you with an audition time next week. You'll need to learn an audition piece this time,' he said to Justine and me. 'Ask Cathy on the way out and she'll give you the scene.'

'Thanks,' I stammered.

Wow! The chance to audition for a speaking role! Just wait till I told Ally and Harriet about this!

In the car on the way home I read the scene that Cathy had given me.

'What's it about?' Mum asked.

'It's between Sara – she's the main character – and Becky, the servant girl, her best friend,' I answered. 'Sara's still rich and she's just come in from a dancing lesson to find Becky asleep in a chair in her room. Instead of being angry with her, she's nice and they start talking and make friends.'

'Which part do you have to learn?' Mum asked.

'The instructions on the top say we can learn either part.' I frowned. 'But I might learn Becky's part. It's more interesting and I bet everyone else will be Sara, because she's the main character.'

'Maybe it would be a good idea to be Becky, then,' Mum agreed. 'It'll make your audition stand out more.'

I nodded. Yes, I'd be Becky.

'I was talking to a few of the other mums while you were out of the room,' Mum told me. 'Some of them had really interesting jobs.'

'What like?' I said.

'One's a journalist, one's started her own jewellery business and Justine's mum owns a clothes shop,' Mum replied. She sighed. 'I felt very boring.'

'You could always change jobs,' I said. 'You could work with animals. That would be loads better than working in an office.'

'I'd love to work with animals,' Mum agreed. 'But what could I do? To be a vet nurse or something like that, you need qualifications.'

'There must be some job with animals you could do,' I said.

Mum frowned thoughtfully. 'Maybe I'll look into it,' she said.

When we got home I jumped out of the car and ran into the house.

Music was coming from Jessica's bedroom. I knocked on her door. 'It's me, Jess.'

She opened the door. 'Soph! How did it go?'

'I've got a second audition!' I said, bouncing into her room and sitting on the bed.

'That's great!' Jess exclaimed.

'I know, and, even better, I've got an audition for a speaking part. If I get it, I'll have some lines to say.'

'Wow!' Jess said, looking very impressed.

I frowned, suddenly feeling that something wasn't right. The music! It was all loud guitars and drums – the sort of thing Tom normally listens to but not Jess. 'What are you listening to?'

'It's Feeder,' Jess replied. 'I like them.'

I stared at her in astonishment. 'Since when?'

'Since . . . just since,' she said, shrugging. 'They're cool.' She turned away. 'I went to hear Tom's band rehearsing today,' she said casually.

'What were they like?' I asked.

'Actually, they were quite good.'

I was very surprised. Tom and Jessica definitely do not like the same kind of music. Jessica likes pop and R'n'B, whereas Tom is into loud music with guitars – the louder the better. In fact, just like the music Jessica had on her CD player right now. 'You really liked them?'

'Zak, the lead singer, is brilliant,' Jess said, nodding. 'He's got an awesome voice.' She sat down on the bed and sighed almost dreamily. 'And he looks like Johnny Depp. He's gorgeous.'

I frowned. It didn't sound like the sort of thing someone who was supposed to be in love with their boyfriend should say.

'He asked me out,' Jessica said, giving me a quick sideways glance.

'What did you say?' I gasped.

'No, of course,' she said quickly. A smile tugged at the corners of her mouth. 'But it was cool that he asked.'

'Did you tell him about Dan?' I demanded.

'Yeah.' She shrugged. 'It didn't seem to put him off though.'

'Sophie!' Mum called up the stairs. 'Harriet's on the phone!'

I went through to Mum and Dad's room and picked up the phone. 'Hi!'

'How was the audition?' Harriet asked eagerly.

I told her all about it.

'That's amazing!' Harriet squealed when I said about the second audition. 'You've got to come round and celebrate.'

'All right.' I grinned. 'I'll come now.'

'I'll get some pens and paper so we can play a game,' I said, and, pulling my sleeping bag around me, I hopped awkwardly over to Harriet's desk. It was only 7.30 but we had already changed ready for bed – me into my lilac cropped pyjamas with stars on, Ally into her sunshine-yellow shorts and strappy-top pyjama set and Harriet in a navy nightshirt. Harriet's fifteen-year-old sister, Emily, was downstairs.

'What shall we play?' Harriet asked as I picked up a pad of paper.

'Consequences,' I said.

'Cool!' Ally exclaimed. 'I love consequences.'

I took three pens from the silver pen-holder. As usual, Harriet's desk was very tidy. Her hairbrush and comb were lined up neatly and her hair bobbles lay in a little silver dish. Along the back of it sat her collection of Beanie Babies and a framed photo of Scooby, her granny's dog.

Harriet's house is our favourite place for sleep-overs. Her bedroom is so small that there's only just room for the three of us in our sleeping bags, but she always has loads of sweets and her dad is brilliant. He never fusses about what time we go to sleep and he always gets us things like Chinese takeways and pizzas to eat.

'This room looks really nice now it's been painted,' Ally commented as I hopped back with the pens and paper.

I nodded, looking round at the pale-blue walls and the silver stars that Harriet and her dad had painted on to the ceiling. 'I wish my room looked like this.'

'At least your room's big,' Harriet told me.

'Yes, but it's not cosy like yours,' I said quickly.

I know Harriet's a bit sensitive about the size of her room. She used to live in a large old house in the village and she had a huge bedroom there, but a year ago her mum and dad got divorced and Harriet and Emily moved to this smaller house with their dad.

I handed out pens and pieces of paper, hoping to change the subject. 'OK,' I said, sitting down between them and making myself comfortable. 'Let's start.'

'Girl's name first?' Harriet asked.

I nodded.

Consequences is one of my all-time favourite games. First you each write a girl's name on a piece of paper and then you fold the paper over so that no one can see what you've written. You pass the paper to the person on your left. Then you write down a boy's name on the new piece of paper and pass it on. Then the place they met, what they might be doing and what the consequences were. At the end you open the pieces of paper and read out what you've got.

'OK, are you ready?' I said, unfolding the piece of paper Harriet had just passed to me. Ally and Harriet nodded. 'Justine Wilcox met Shrek up a mountain,' I read out. 'They played tennis and the consequence was that we all get level fours in our SATs.'

We giggled.

'My turn! My turn!' Ally cried. 'This is a really good

one. Miss Carter met Brad Pitt by the post office. They did cartwheels and the consequence was that they had a baby!'

We all burst out laughing.

'Here's mine,' Harriet said quickly. 'Ally —' she grinned at Ally — 'met Snowy the Beanie Baby in the bus shelter. They snogged and the consequence was they got married and ran away together!'

We all shrieked with laughter.

'Your true love, Ally!' I gasped.

'You're meant for each other,' Harriet cried.

Ally leapt out of her sleeping bag and grabbed Snowy, the polar bear Beanie Baby, off the desk. 'Marry me, Snowy!' she said dramatically.

'Can I be bridesmaid?' I cried.

'And me?' Harriet gasped.

Suddenly the door flew open. Our laughter stopped abruptly.

Emily was standing there, looking furious. 'For goodness' sake!' she exclaimed. 'You lot are so irritating. Do you *have* to make so much noise!'

There was a moment's pause. I saw Harriet's face fall and then Ally made the Beanie toy jump up and down and squeaked in a little voice, 'Yes, I will marry you, Ally. I will!'

That was it. Laughter just exploded out of me, and as soon as I started laughing, Ally and Harriet did too. We rolled around the floor, clutching our sides.

Emily looked like she didn't know what to do, so she contented herself with shooting us a filthy look. 'You're pathetic, you know that! You should just –' she struggled for words – 'grow up!' And with that, she swung round and stalked away.

My sides ached, but I couldn't stop laughing. I am *so* glad I don't have Emily for a sister!

Chapter Four

I'll get the part, I thought. I swallowed. It was 2.10 on Saturday afternoon and, once again, Mum and I were sitting in the waiting room with its plastic orange chairs and faint smell of sweaty feet. Around the room four girls were sitting tensely with their mums or dads. There was definitely less of a relaxed atmosphere than the week before.

I'll get the part, I thought determinedly. I'd read in one of Jessica's magazines about the power of positive thinking. It said that if you want something really badly, you should imagine yourself getting it and if you think it hard enough then you will get it. I had never wanted anything so much as I wanted a speaking part in the film and so I was determined to be as positive as I could.

I looked at the door. Justine had gone in for her audition five minutes ago. I was next.

I will get the part, I thought, taking a deep breath and trying to be confident, like the magazine had suggested. *I will definitely get the part.* It was working: I felt calm and in control . . .

The door opened. My tummy did a double-flip.

'What if I forget my lines?' I squeaked to Mum, positive thinking flying out of the window as my body turned to a trembling jelly.

'You won't,' Mum said reassuringly. 'You've been practising all week. You'll be just fine.'

Justine looked very relieved to have the audition over. She hurried to her mum.

'OK. Can I have Sophie Tennison next please?' Cathy said, consulting her list.

I stood up and Mum squeezed my hand.

Cathy smiled at me. 'This way, Sophie.'

My heart thumped in my chest as I followed her to the audition room. This time there were three people in there – Steve, whom I'd met last time, a woman about my mum's age and an older man.

The woman, who was smartly dressed in an olive-green suit, spoke first. 'Hello, Sophie. I'm Sheila Blake, the casting director. You know Steve –' Steve smiled at me – 'and this is Laurence Derrington, the film's director.'

I looked at the older man. He was sitting deep in his chair. He was about fifty, with a beard, greying hair and thick eyebrows that looked like big grey caterpillars perched above his dark eyes. He was wearing jeans and a white T-shirt.

'What we'd like you to do is to go through the scene you've learned,' Sheila said. 'I'll read in the other lines in the scene. Which part have you chosen?'

'Becky,' I said.

I sensed all the adults stir slightly in surprise. Laurence Derrington seemed to sit up and look at me more closely.

'You're the first person who's chosen Becky,' Sheila said. 'Well, if you'd like to go into the middle of the room, use the chair that's there. Just take your time and start when you're ready.'

I took a deep breath and went over to the chair. It was old-fashioned, with a high back and arms. Feeling horribly aware of Laurence, Sheila and Steve watching me, I sat down and curled my legs up. Shutting my eyes, I concentrated hard and tried to forget the watching adults. I was Becky, not Sophie. I wasn't in an audition. I'd been up since 4 o'clock in the morning, sweeping out fireplaces, carrying coal, scrubbing floors. I hadn't had any breakfast. I was hungry, dirty and very, very tired.

There was a moment's silence when the only sound in the room seemed to be the thudding of my heart, and then Sheila, pretending to be Sara, said the first line.

'Oh, look. The poor thing. She's fallen asleep. If Miss Minchin finds her she'll be very cross. What should I do?'

I gave a gasp and jumped up. 'Oh, Miss. I'm sorry, really I am,' I cried. 'I didn't mean to do it. It was just the warm fire and me being so tired and all.'

The words tumbled out. I forgot about being

nervous. In fact, I forgot I was being watched. I know it sounds weird, but it was almost like I wasn't me, like I was living a different life for a while.

At the end of the scene, I paused and blinked. The world slowly came back into focus. I wasn't sitting in an old-fashioned bedroom, looking at a girl in a beautiful white dress. I was in an audition room, being watched by three people.

I looked up. All the adults were sitting up in their chairs, staring at me.

'That . . . that was really extremely good,' Laurence said, almost as if he was surprised. 'Come and sit down a minute, Sophie.' He pointed to a chair in front of the desk.

I walked over. I was feeling mega-relieved that I hadn't got any lines wrong.

'So, tell me,' Laurence said. 'Why did you choose the part of Becky?'

'I . . . I just liked it more,' I replied as I sat down. 'I mean, I know Sara's the main part, but in that part of the story she's a bit boring. I thought it would be more interesting to be Becky.'

'Well, it was a very good performance,' Laurence said.

He stared at me intently without saying anything for a moment. I felt myself going red. What was he looking at me like that for? Why wasn't he saying anything?

Suddenly he held out his script. 'Would you mind reading another of Becky's scenes for us?'

Would I mind! I shook my head and took the script.

'Page sixty-seven. Go to the middle and have a quick read through,' Laurence said. 'When you're ready we'll start. Sheila will read in Sara's words again.'

I did as he said. As I read through the scene, I noticed that the adults were leaning together and talking in low voices. I could only make out a little of what they were saying. 'A real wistfulness . . .' I heard Laurence say. 'And those eyes . . .' His voice dropped quieter and I couldn't hear any more.

'I'm ready,' I said at last.

The scene was only short and, after I had finished it, Laurence asked me to try a few lines again with a different expression.

I did as he asked and he seemed pleased. 'Great,' he said, smiling as I finished. 'That was spot on. Well done.'

Sheila stood up. 'Who brought you here today, Sophie?'

'My mum,' I replied.

'We'd like to speak to her,' Sheila said.

I followed her and Cathy out of the room.

'You were a long time,' Mum said, standing up as I walked into the waiting room. Her eyes scanned my face. 'How did it go?'

Before I could answer, Sheila stepped forward. 'Mrs Tennison, my name is Sheila Blake,' she said. 'I'm the casting director for the film. The director and I would like to have a word with you.'

Mum looked surprised. 'With me?'

Sheila nodded.

Mum followed her to the door. I went after her, but Cathy stopped me. 'Sheila and Laurence want to speak to your mum on her own, Sophie. Do you mind waiting here?'

Feeling more confused than ever, I sat down. What was going on? No one else's mum had been asked to speak to Laurence and Sheila. I looked at the floor. *Please*, I thought, *please let it mean they're giving me a speaking part. Even just one line!*

As soon as I heard the door open I jumped to my feet. Mum came in. She looked shocked.

'What did they say?' I demanded.

'I . . . I think you'd better come and speak to them yourself,' she said.

✦

Chapter Five

'Hi, Sophie,' Sheila said as I followed Mum into the audition room. 'Has your mum told you why we spoke to her?'

I shook my head. *What's going on?* I wanted to shout.

'Well, we were all very impressed. We're definitely going to offer you a speaking part . . .'

Yes! I had a speaking part! I was going to be in the film and say some lines! How amazing was that? Just wait till . . .

'And we would also like to screen-test you for the role of Becky.'

My whirling thoughts stopped in their tracks. I stared at Sheila. *What* had she just said?

'A screen test is like an audition but it's in costume and it's filmed,' Sheila went on mega-calmly. 'It gives us an idea of what you'd actually be like playing the part on film.'

'Becky!' I squeaked. 'You . . . you want *me* to audition for Becky!'

Laurence nodded. 'We've been auditioning lots of young actresses,' he explained. 'But we haven't found

Becky yet. You understand this isn't a definite offer, it's just that we'd like to see you again.'

Every single word in my brain seemed to have deserted me. I nodded speechlessly.

'You'll need to do the scene you prepared for today and this scene as well,' Sheila said, passing it across the desk. 'The screen test will take place just outside London.' She smiled at Mum. 'We'll send you all the details, Mrs Tennison. Thank you very much for bringing Sophie in.' She turned to me. 'We'll look forward to seeing you next week, Sophie.'

A minute later Mum and I were standing in the corridor outside. We stared at each other.

'Well . . .' Mum said, totally lost for words.

'I'm going to audition for Becky.' As it started to sink in, a grin plastered itself across my face. 'Oh, wow! Wait till everyone hears about this!'

On the way home, Mum tried to persuade me that it might be a good idea to keep quiet about my screen test. 'We'll have to tell Dad and Tom and Jessica,' she said. 'And I know you'll want to talk to Ally and Harriet about it, but I do think it might be best if you didn't mention it to anyone else.'

I stared at her. The most amazing thing ever had happened and Mum wanted me to keep quiet!

'Why?' I said.

'Well, just in case you don't get the part,' Mum said.

'After all, it's only another audition. They said they've been looking at lots of people to find someone to play Becky. There's no guarantee you'll be chosen.'

'But I might be,' I said quickly.

Mum nodded. 'Still, until you know for sure, isn't it best not to go about telling everyone?'

'But I *want* to tell people,' I protested. I thought of something. 'Anyway, Justine's bound to ask me how the audition went. You don't want me to lie, do you?'

I could tell I'd got Mum there. There was no way she would ever say I should lie.

'No, I suppose not,' Mum said reluctantly. She sighed. 'Well, OK, tell people if you must, only don't get too excited.'

Me? Get too excited? Never!

'I'm going to London for a screen test!' I shouted, running into the kitchen. Seeing Dad and Jessica, I hugged Dad in excitement. 'The director wants me to audition for Becky! I could have one of the biggest parts in the film!'

'What?' Dad said in astonishment.

I repeated my news.

'They want you to audition for a main part?' Jessica echoed.

I nodded. 'Isn't it amazing?'

'Yes.' Jessica sounded rather stunned. 'Yes, it is.'

Just then, Mum came into the kitchen. 'So you've

heard. It's, er . . . a surprise, isn't it?' she said to Dad.

'I can't believe it,' Jessica said, looking at me as if I was an alien. 'You might be a film star!'

'It's only another audition, Jessica,' Mum said quickly. 'They're been seeing lots of people. Sophie is very unlikely to get the part.'

'But I *might* get it.' I twirled round. I felt like singing, like dancing, like jumping up and down. 'I might be a film star!' I said, hugging Dad again.

Dad hugged me back, but over my head I could tell he was looking at Mum. 'What would it mean in practice?' he asked, his arms tightening round me almost protectively.

'Well, Sophie would be filming for most of the summer,' Mum answered. 'It would be a big-time commitment – there'd be lots of travelling, and she'd be away filming on location for a while –'

'Can I ring Ally and Harriet?' I interrupted, breaking away from Dad. I couldn't wait to tell them my news!

Mum nodded and I raced to the phone.

I phoned Harriet first. She was totally astonished. 'That's so cool' she gasped. 'Oh, Soph, you're going to be famous!'

A broad grin split my face. 'I haven't got the part yet.'

'No, but you will get it,' Harriet said. 'I just know you will. This is so amazing! We've got to have a sleepover to celebrate. I'll go and ask if you and Ally can come over.'

A few minutes later, she came back on the phone. 'Dad said yes,' she told me. 'I'll ring Ally. Do you want to come over now?'

Harriet, Ally and I hardly talked about anything else but my screen test for the whole of the evening. In fact, I hardly even thought about anything else for the next few days. But all that changed on Wednesday night, when Mum announced some news.

Jessica, Tom and I were in the kitchen after school. Jessica and Tom were arguing. They argue with each other much more than with me.

'That's my baseball cap,' Jessica said, reaching out and swiping the grey cord cap off Tom's head.

'You said I could have it,' Tom said, quickly ruffling his flattened brown hair so it stood up in spikes again.

'Borrow it, not have it,' Jessica said. She looked inside it. 'Eee – gross! You've got gel in it, Tom.'

'You've got gel in it, Tom,' Tom mimicked.

Jessica shot him a withering look, but before she could say anything Mum and Dad came into the kitchen.

'You're home early, Dad,' I said.

'That's because your mother and I have got some news,' Dad said.

I looked at Mum. 'What news?'

Jessica glanced at Mum's excited face and a look of intense alarm entered her eyes. 'You're not having a baby! Please don't tell me you're having a baby, Mum!'

'Of course I'm not having a baby.' Mum laughed.

'So what's going on?' Tom asked.

'Sit down, all of you,' Dad said in his calm voice.

We sat down, exchanging glances.

'OK,' Mum said, taking a deep breath. 'Well, I think you all know I've not been happy in my job for a while. So I've decided that enough's enough. I'm –' the words rushed out of her – 'I'm going to start a business.'

We all stared.

'What sort of business?' Tom asked.

Mum's eyes shone. 'A pet-sitting business.'

'Pet-sitting!' Jessica exclaimed. 'That's when you look after other people's animals when they go away on holiday, isn't it?'

Mum nodded. 'Some of the pets will come here and sometimes I'll go to their houses to stay.' She looked round at us. 'So, what do you all think?'

'It's a brilliant idea!' I exclaimed. I loved the idea of having animals to stay.

'Yeah!' Jessica agreed. 'The more animals the better.'

Tom nodded.

'I'll try and build up the business so that I can employ someone else to do the staying away,' Mum said. 'But at first I'm going to have to do the overnight stays.'

'Mum the businesswoman!' Tom grinned.

Mum looked almost dazed. 'There's going to be so much to do.'

Dad put his arm round Mum's shoulders. 'Well, we're all here to help you.'

We nodded.

Mum looked almost teary for a moment. 'Thank you,' she said. She cleared her throat. 'Now, how about some coffee and biscuits to celebrate?'

'So, have you thought of a name for your business, Mum?' Jessica asked as Dad put the kettle on.

Mum smiled. 'Purr-fect for Pets!' she said.

Chapter Six

'Keep your eyes closed. That's it. Just a sweep of shadow here . . . and here . . .'

It was the day of the screen test and I was sitting in a small room in front of a mirror, my eyes shut while Jules, a hair and make-up artist, applied eyeshadow with a tickly brush.

'Now open,' Jules told me. She was very pretty, with long red hair clipped up in a slide.

I opened my eyes. The room was white and lights seemed to blaze at me from all directions. My eyelashes felt prickly. I blinked several times and looked in the mirror on the wall in front of me. My eyes looked enormous! Jules had applied mascara to my eyelashes and eyeliner round my eyes. She'd also put foundation on my face and a little blusher.

'OK, up you get,' she said.

I stood up and Jules removed the gown that had been protecting my costume.

'So, what do you think?' she said as I looked in the mirror.

I stared at my reflection. Was it really me? My hair

was pinned up under a white maid's cap. I was wearing a dirty white shirt, a long black skirt, thick black tights and boots.

'Do you feel like Becky?' Jules asked.

'Yes,' I said slowly. 'I do.'

My heart pitter-pattered with excitement. I knew the scenes. I looked like Becky. This was it: my big chance!

Laurence, Sheila and Steve were all waiting for me.

'Hi,' Sheila said as Mum and I went in. 'Mrs Tennison, if you'd like to come and sit over here.' She showed Mum to a chair at the side of the room where the screen test was taking place.

I clutched the scenes, feeling suddenly nervous.

Laurence smiled at me. 'We'll have a couple of rehearsals and then we'll start filming. Now, if you come over here, Sophie.'

I followed him over to the set.

'We'll start with the scene that you did last week for us. I'd like you to curl up in that chair and pretend to be asleep. Sheila will read Sara's lines again. She'll be sitting just to the right of that camera.'

I looked round and saw Sheila now sitting beside one of the cameras.

'Try not to look into the camera,' Laurence said. 'Just say your lines directly to Sheila.'

Taking a deep breath, I went to the chair and sat

down. The camera seemed very close to me. I forced myself to ignore it.

I can do this, I thought, closing my eyes.

Sheila read Sara's lines and I pretended to wake up.

'Oh, Miss. I'm sorry, really I am,' I gasped, looking straight at Sheila. 'I didn't mean to do it.'

I continued for a few lines and then Laurence asked me to stop.

'I'd like you to start moving now,' he said. 'If you just stay in the same place it gets a bit boring.' He looked round the set, as if trying to think of something for me to do.

I had an idea. 'I could pick up the coal brush,' I suggested. 'Becky's gone to sleep really suddenly, hasn't she? Well, maybe she left the brush on the floor and now she sees it and picks it up, because she's scared she'll get into more trouble.'

'Good idea,' Laurence said, nodding.

I felt great as I saw the approval in his eyes. Confidence bubbled up inside me. This was fun!

We finished the scene and ran through it once more so I was sure of what I was doing, and then I had to make something called a slate. That just meant standing in front of a camera and saying my name, age and height. I smiled into the camera and spoke as clearly as I could.

'Great,' Laurence said. 'Now, let's start filming.'

After finishing the scene, I rehearsed the next scene and then that was filmed.

'Excellent!' Laurence said.

'That was all really good,' Sheila said, smiling at me. 'Now, if you can just give me and Laurence a few minutes together.'

While they talked, I went over to Mum.

Steve joined us. 'Well done,' he said.

I smiled at him. 'Thanks.'

'You really have learned the scenes well,' he said. 'You didn't need any prompting – not even in the rehearsal. That's very unusual.'

'I like learning lines,' I said.

Mum smiled. 'I think Sophie knows every single word of those two scenes – both Becky's and Sara's.'

I nodded. 'I do.'

'Go on, then,' Steve said, grinning at me. 'Do Sara's lines.'

I could tell he thought I wouldn't really know them. But I did. So I sat down on the floor and started the scene I had just done but saying Sara's lines. The scene began with Sara speaking to her pet rat, Melchisedec, in her attic bedroom before Becky came in.

'It's been hard today, Melchisedec,' I started, imagining I was holding Melchisedec in my hands. 'Harder than usual.'

As I spoke, I felt my voice and body change from

how I acted when I was being Becky. Becky was always scared, like a little mouse, hurrying and scurrying. Sara was different, tired and hungry, but very proud. I shivered and drew the pretend rat closer.

'It's been a cold afternoon and it's going to be a cold night. And today Lavinia laughed at me for having mud on my skirt. It's very hard trying to be a princess and I wish, oh, I just wish . . .'

I swallowed and dropped my head on to my knees. 'Oh, Papa,' I whispered, imagining what it would be like if it was my own dad who'd died. 'What a long, long time it seems since you hugged me last.'

Suddenly I became aware that Laurence had stopped talking to Sheila and was staring at me.

'That's Sara.' The words shot out of him as he walked over, his eyes like dark beetles under his thick grey eyebrows.

I felt suddenly uncomfortable. 'I . . . I just learned the lines for fun,' I stammered, getting up. I hadn't done anything wrong, had I? Was he cross with me?

'Do it again,' Laurence said intently.

I looked around. 'Here?'

'No,' Laurence said. 'On the set. Sheila!' He glanced round. 'Watch Sophie do this speech.'

I walked over to the set. What was going on? Taking a deep breath, I tried to concentrate. *Sara*, I thought. *Don't think about anything else. Just be Sara.* Letting my breath out, I started at the first line and only stopped when I reached the end of the speech. I looked up. Now *everyone* was staring at me.

'Excuse us a minute,' Laurence said, glancing at Sheila and Steve.

I nodded and they all hurried through to a little room at the back of the main room and shut the door. I could see them start to talk. Laurence seemed excited.

I went over to Mum. 'What's going on?' I said uncertainly. 'What are they talking about?'

'I don't know,' she said. 'But you did that speech very well.'

I bit my lip. Well, surely that meant things were OK, then, didn't it?

At that moment, Laurence came out of the room. 'Would you mind doing the whole scene for us – as Sara?' he asked me. 'We'd like to film it.'

Film it! This was beyond weird! Still, if that's what they wanted, I'd do it.

'OK,' I said.

And so I went through the whole scene again, but this time with Sheila reading in Becky's lines.

At the end, there was a long pause. I looked at Laurence. He was nodding slowly. He looked deep in thought.

I got to my feet. 'Do you want me to do anything else?'

'No, that will be fine,' Laurence said. He cleared his throat. 'Now, we should let you get out of costume,' he said, his voice suddenly brisk. 'Steve will take you back down to the dressing room.' He stepped forward and held out his hand. 'Thank you so much for coming in today, Sophie.'

I shook his hand. What about the part? Was I Becky or wasn't I?

Sheila seemed to read my thoughts. 'We've got other people coming in for screen tests this afternoon,' she explained. 'But we'll be in touch in the next few days, once we've made a decision.'

I couldn't believe it. A few days! I couldn't wait that long to find out.But it looked as if I was going to have to.

Mum shook hands with Laurence and Sheila and that was it. We left the studio and headed down the long white corridors back to the dressing room. Inside I felt a sinking feeling, as if I were a balloon going down.

It was over and I didn't know if I'd got the part. How much of an anticlimax was that? After having to read the part of Sara and all the things they'd asked me to do! I hardly said a word as I got changed.

'How are you feeling, sweetheart?' Mum asked as we left the building and walked to the car.

I shrugged. 'Don't know.' In fact, I felt as flat as a piece of paper.

Mum squeezed my hand. 'It's only a few days until you find out.' She smiled. 'Tell you what, why don't we get a McDonald's on the way home?'

*

By the time I had eaten a quarterpounder with cheese, fries and a strawberry milkshake and Mum had stopped at an out-of-town shopping centre and bought me a really cool black top with the word ANGEL written across it in silver sequins, the dying balloon feeling had gone and I was almost cheerful again.

'It was brilliant going to a real film studio, wasn't it?' I said to Mum as we drove home.

'It was certainly different,' she said.

'Do you think I'll get to be Becky?' I asked.

'I don't know, love, but you did really well. You mustn't be disappointed if you don't get the part.'

I thought about the screen test. It was strange to think that other girls would be going into the dressing room, putting on the same clothes as me and saying the same lines. How good would they be? Probably really, really good.

Suddenly I began to wish that I'd followed Mum's advice and kept quiet about the screen test. Everyone at school knew about it. What was it going to be like if I didn't get the part? Justine Wilcox would be the first to gloat. She'd been mega-fed up when she'd heard about the screen test. I groaned inwardly. Oh, no, this could be *so* embarrassing!

When Mum and I got home at 5 o'clock, Jessica came downstairs.

'How did the screen test go?' she asked eagerly.

'Fine,' Mum said. 'Really well.' She sat down with a sigh. 'My feet.'

Jessica took a heavy cardboard box off the dresser. She carried it over and plonked it down in front of Mum. 'Ta-da!'

'What's this?' Mum asked.

'Purr-fect for Pets brochures!' Jessica said. 'Dad collected them this morning.' She opened the top and took out a glossy folded brochure. 'Don't they look brilliant?'

I hurried over. They did look good. On the front cover was a big purple title saying 'Purr-fect for Pets' and four small photographs of Wilson, Baxter, Milly the rabbit and Pickles the guinea pig.

'I could drop them in at people's houses when I do my paper round this evening,' Jessica offered as Mum picked one up.

Mum nodded. 'That would be great. Thanks, Jess.' She stared at the brochure in her hand. 'It looks so official. So real.'

'It is real,' I said, hugging her. 'You've got your own business, Mum!'

Mum smiled. 'Now all I need is some clients.'

Brrring brrring . . . brrring brrring . . .

I blinked my eyes open. The phone was ringing. I looked at my bedside clock. It was only 8.15. Practically the middle of the night.

Brrring brrring . . . brrring brrring . . .

I turned over and buried my face in the pillow. There was no way I was getting up. I wondered why Dad didn't answer it. Unlike the rest of us, he was happy first thing in the morning and was usually up and about by 7.30. Maybe he'd gone out on his bike.

Brrring brrring . . .

Go away! I thought, and then suddenly I sat bolt upright as the events of the day before flooded back to me. The phone! Maybe it was the film company!

I leapt out of bed, half falling as the duvet cover tangled around my feet. Scrambling for the door, I raced down the stairs and grabbed the phone from the table in the hall.

'Hello, who is it please?' I gasped, my heart pounding.

A woman spoke. 'Hello, my name's Mrs Lorrimer. I'm ringing about pet-sitting.'

The breath left me in a rush of disappointment. 'I'll . . . I'll just get my mum,' I said.

Mum was already coming down the stairs in her dressing gown. I handed her the phone. 'It's about pets,' I said.

Leaving Mum to talk to the woman, I went through to the kitchen. As soon as I opened the door, Baxter and Wilson trotted over, their tails wagging and their mouths open in big doggy grins as they pushed themselves against my legs.

'Hi there,' I said, scratching their ears.

I opened the door to let them out. Dad's bike and cycle helmet had gone. It looked like my guess had been right. He was out getting some exercise. Totally mad!

I poured myself a glass of orange juice and sat down. Should I go back to bed? No, I decided. The shock of thinking the phone call might be from Laurence or Sheila had left me well and truly awake. Baxter trotted in and laid his head on my knee and looked up at me with big hopeful eyes.

I kissed his head. 'You want to go for a walk?'

Baxter jumped up and pricked his ears in excitement. Hearing the magic word 'walk', Wilson raced in from outside, his tail wagging madly.

Draining my orange juice, I went upstairs and pulled on some clothes. The dogs were waiting eagerly by the back door. I was just fixing on their leads when Mum replaced the receiver.

'Well, I think I might have just spoken to my first customer,' she said, looking pleased. 'Mrs Lorrimer – the lady on the phone – has got a dog she wants looking after. She's going to come round later this morning to meet me.'

'That's brilliant,' I said.

Mum looked round at the kitchen. The floor was scattered with dog toys and a chewed-up newspaper that Wilson or Baxter had demolished in the night. 'I think

I'd better start tidying up,' she said with a sigh. 'Are you taking the dogs out?'

I nodded.

'What about breakfast?'

'I'll have some when I get back.'

I headed out. Curtains were still drawn across windows and the roads, which were usually full of cars at this time of day in the week, were quiet. Wilson and Baxter trotted along beside me as we headed for the recreation ground. It all seemed so normal. It made the day before feel like a dream. Had I really spent yesterday morning at a film studio doing a screen test? I thought about the film. If I was Becky, I'd get to spend all summer acting. I'd meet famous people and I'd probably be on TV and in magazines.

Oh, please, I prayed, crossing my fingers so hard that it hurt. *Let me get the part.*

'Has anyone phoned?' I asked as soon as I got home.

Mum was mopping the floor, so I left the dogs outside.

'I've had another call about Purr-fect for Pets,' she said. 'There's a lady with twelve rabbits she wants me to look after next weekend.'

'Twelve rabbits. Wow, that's great,' I said, trying to sound enthusiastic to hide my disappointment that there had been no phone calls from the film company.

Mum looked up and I could tell I hadn't fooled her.

'You know you probably won't hear anything about the film today, Sophie – Sheila did say a few days.'

So much for disguising my thoughts! 'I know,' I sighed. I started helping her set up for breakfast. 'I just hate all this waiting. Why can't they let me know?'

'They're not going to make a snap decision over something so important,' Mum said. She looked at me with a worried expression on her face. 'You're not going to be too upset if you don't get it, are you? Remember, the others trying out will have lots more experience than you.'

I didn't say anything.

'You'll be in the film, that's the most important thing,' Mum said.

But it wasn't. I wanted to be Becky. I wanted to be the one people knew and recognized. I poured some Frosties and milk into a bowl. But I didn't feel like eating. I swirled the orange flakes around with my spoon.

Jessica came downstairs in her pyjamas. 'Any Purrfect for Pets phone calls?' she asked Mum.

'Two,' Mum said, and started talking about her prospective clients with the dog and the rabbits.

Just then Dad arrived back from his bike ride. 'Morning, all!' he said cheerily. He put the Sunday papers down on the table and sighed happily. 'Breakfast! Excellent! I feel like bacon.'

In next to no time, he had the packet of bacon out of

the fridge and the grill on. 'Bacon butties all round?' he asked, laying rashers of bacon under the grill.

We all nodded and soon the delicious smell of grilling bacon was wafting through the house. It even brought Tom down from his bedroom — a miracle, seeing as he doesn't normally come out of his room until at least 11 o'clock at weekends.

'Bacon! Can I have some?' he asked, yawning as he staggered into the kitchen in his boxer shorts and dressing gown.

It was then that the phone started to ring.

'I'll get it,' Mum said. 'It might be another call for Purr-fect for Pets.' She picked up the phone. 'Annie Tennison speaking.'

I watched her face. Who was it this time — a person with a dog, a cat, maybe a pony?

'Oh, yes, hello,' Mum said, her tone changing suddenly. I could tell that she knew the person on the other end of the line. She glanced swiftly at me. 'Yes, she's here. I'll just get her.' She held out the phone, her hand covering the mouthpiece. 'Sophie, it's for you. It's Sheila Blake.'

Chapter Seven

I stared at Mum. This was it: the phone call I'd been waiting for! I was about to run and grab the phone when suddenly I froze. What if I hadn't got the part?

'Sophie!' Mum said, holding out the phone.

'Go on,' Jess urged.

Feeling sick, I walked slowly over to Mum. My fingers curled round the receiver. 'H . . . hello.'

'Sophie, hi. It's Sheila.' The casting director's deep rich voice filled my ear. 'I've got some news for you.'

My chest felt tight. 'Yes,' I whispered.

'Well, we're not offering you the part of Becky . . .'

The breath left me in a rush. I hadn't got the part. Tears prickled in my eyes. I had never felt so disappointed in my entire life.

'But,' Sheila continued, 'we would like to offer you the part of Sara.'

There was a pause.

I blinked. What had Sheila just said?

'Sophie?'

'P . . . pardon?' I stammered.

'We'd like you to play Sara,' Sheila repeated.

'But . . . but I didn't audition for Sara,' I said stupidly. She couldn't mean it. It was some sort of mistake.

'I know you didn't,' Sheila said. 'We've only been auditioning young actresses with previous experience for the role. But that last scene you did as Sara at your screen test yesterday just blew everyone away. You're very talented. You managed to get exactly the mix of wistfulness, dignity and courage that we've been looking for. We all agreed you're perfect for the role, so the part's yours – if you want it.'

Want it! My brain kicked into gear. 'I do!' I gasped.

'Great,' Sheila replied, and I could hear the smile in her voice. 'Well, can you put your mum back on the phone. We've got quite a lot to sort out.'

I looked round and realized that my family were all staring at me, their faces showing a mixture of tension, concern and hope.

'Well?' Jessica demanded. 'What's happening? Did you get the part?'

'I . . . I'm going to be Sara,' I said, grinning. My voice rose. 'It's the main part!'

'What?' Jessica gasped.

I held out the receiver to Mum. 'Sheila wants to talk to you.'

Looking stunned, Mum took the phone. 'Hello,' she said, and, giving me an astonished look, she carried the receiver through to the next room.

'You're the main part?' Dad said.

'Yes.' As I spoke, I realized it was true. I grabbed his hands and jumped up and down. 'I'm going to be Sara!' I cried. 'I'm going to be Sara!'

'You'll be famous,' Jessica said in astonishment.

'This is totally weird,' Tom said. He shook his head. 'But, you know, like, well done, Soph.'

'Thanks!' I said, racing over and hugging him.

Tom looked very surprised. We never hug normally. But I was so excited I'd have hugged a gorilla if it had been standing in the kitchen – come to think of it, maybe there isn't much difference!

'I just can't believe it!' I exclaimed, breaking free and twirling over to hug Jessica. I was going to be Sara! What could be cooler or better than that!

Mum came back through to the kitchen. She looked totally stunned.

'Is it true?' Dad said.

'Of course it's true!' I said.

Mum nodded. 'Bill Armstrong, the producer, is going to drive up to see us on Wednesday afternoon. He'll bring the contracts, script and information about filming.' She looked at me. 'Sheila said Sophie was very talented.'

'She told me that too,' I said, feeling a wave of pride.

'And did she say what a very big head you have?' Jessica teased.

I picked up a Frostie from the table and threw it at her.

'Missed!' she cried, grinning as she ducked.

'I can't believe it,' Mum said, hurrying over and hugging me. 'You've done so well, Sophie. My little girl in a film! My baby!'

'Mum!' I protested, wriggling away.

Just then the phone rang.

Tom got it. 'Mum, it's for you,' he said. 'Purr-fect for Pets.'

'Another call!' Mum said. She smiled at me. 'Looks like both our dreams are coming true.'

I went straight round to Harriet's. Ally was there and they were about to go riding. When I told them my news they both squealed with excitement and hugged me – I didn't think I'd ever had so many hugs in one day!

'So, will you have loads of lines to learn?' Ally said.

'Loads.' I nodded. 'The producer's bringing the script round on Wednesday.'

'The producer! That sounds really weird,' Ally said.

Harriet's forehead creased. 'You'll still be friends with us, won't you?'

'Definitely not,' I teased. 'I'll only associate with other famous people.'

Ally swung her riding hat at me.

I grinned and dodged. 'You just won't be cool enough

for me!' I said, and then I had to turn and run as both Ally and Harriet chased after me, swinging their hats.

'Truce! Truce!' I begged as they cornered me by the gate.

They gave in.

'I guess we'd better not injure a film star,' Ally said. She smiled. 'This really is so cool, Soph.'

'Yeah! Just wait till you tell everyone at school!' Harriet grinned.

Monday was brilliant. I told Miss Carter about getting the part and she told everyone else. Most people seemed really pleased for me. Justine, of course, wasn't.

'Why you?' she said, confronting me in the playground at break time. 'I mean, it's not like you're anything special.'

I wanted to say, 'Because I can act,' but I ignored her and walked past.

'I see. We're not good enough to talk to now, are we?' Justine called after me. 'You're such a snob, Sophie Tennison!'

'I am not!' I said, swinging round.

'You are so. Always thinking you're better than everyone else.'

'I don't think that,' I protested.

'How much are you going to get paid?' Saskia, Justine's friend, asked.

'I'm not telling,' I replied.

In fact, Dad had said that although I could have a hundred pounds to spend, the rest was to be put away into a savings account for when I was older.

'Go on. Tell us,' Saskia said.

'No. Mind your own business.' I walked off. Why did they have to be so horrid?

'Snob!' Justine called after me.

'Idiot!' Ally muttered as she and Harriet caught up with me.

'She's just jealous,' Harriet said, taking my arm. 'Come on. Take no notice. Let's go and sit on the wall.'

Over the next few days, the phone seemed to be constantly ringing with relatives and friends wanting to congratulate me. Mum must have told the whole world! On Tuesday afternoon a journalist from the local paper came to interview me about how it felt to get the part and then on Wednesday the film's producer, Bill Armstrong, drove up from London. Dad had come home from work early to meet him.

Bill was in his fifties, with short greying hair. Wearing cream trousers and a blue shirt, he looked disappointingly normal. I'd imagined that a film producer would be very cool and fashionable, not like someone from Dad's accountancy office.

We went to the dining room and, while Bill talked about the contract with Mum and Dad, I flicked through a copy of the script he'd given me. I was in almost every scene. I was going to have loads of lines to learn! My stomach flipped over. What if I got things wrong?

Bill gave Mum an application form for a performing licence to fill in.

'All children have to have a licence from their local education authority if they are going to work professionally,' he explained. 'If you can fill in the details now, I'll send it off this week.'

He looked through his papers and handed me a typed sheet.

'This is the basic shooting schedule, Sophie. It gives you a rough idea of when and where scenes will be filmed. You'll see we don't film them in order,' he said as I looked at the schedule and saw that on the first day scenes twelve, fifteen and twenty-six were being shot. 'We try and film all the scenes that take place on the same set at the same time. It saves money because we don't have to keep rebuilding the set.'

'Where will the filming take place?' Dad asked.

'We start with five weeks at Stanton Hall. It's a boarding school about twenty minutes away from here. By the time we start filming, the school will have broken up. After that there's a week's filming in Lincolnshire, followed by four weeks at a film-studio complex near Birmingham. Sophie shouldn't be needed for all four of those weeks. We are aiming to film all the scenes with children in during the summer holidays if we possibly can,' he told Mum and Dad. 'Now,' he went on, 'we need to talk about chaperons. All children on a film set have to be chaperoned by an adult. Parents can be chaperons, but in general we prefer to employ professionals. The chaperons we use are all very experienced and understand about the demands of filming. However, it's up to you. If you prefer, you can chaperon Sophie yourselves.'

'I don't think we'd able to,' Dad said. 'My wife's just starting a new business and I work full-time.' He looked at me. 'Would you be happy to be looked after by one of the company's chaperons, Sophie?'

'I guess,' I said rather nervously.

Bill smiled at me. 'Don't worry. You'll like them. By the end of the filming they'll be like an extra mum to you.' He looked at Mum and Dad. 'But maybe one of you could act as Sophie's chaperon for the script read-through and possibly the first day's rehearsal,' he suggested. 'Just while Sophie gets to know everyone. After that I'm sure she'll feel very much at home.'

Mum nodded. 'That makes sense.'

At last everything was agreed.

Dad saw Bill to his car. Jessica and Dan were sitting in the kitchen.

'So that was the film's producer?' Jessica said.

I nodded.

'He looked really normal,' Jessica said, sounding disappointed.

71

'He was normal,' I said, sitting down at the table. 'Just like Dad.'

'I can't believe you're going to be in a film,' Dan said, looking at me strangely. 'I mean, you're you, Sophie. And you're going to be a film star!'

I grinned. 'I know. Isn't it brilliant!'

Dan stood up. 'Well, I'd better go. I'm supposed to be seeing my gran tonight. I'll see you tomorrow,' he said to Jessica. 'Shall we go to Matt's? He's getting some videos in.'

I saw Jessica frown slightly. 'Again. Can't we do something else?'

'Like what?' Dan said. 'I'm broke.'

'Me too,' Jessica admitted. She sighed. 'OK, I guess Matt's it is, then.'

They kissed quickly and Dan left. Jessica sat down at the table. She looked fed up.

'What's the matter?' I asked.

'Nothing,' she replied. 'It's just we always either hang out here or seem go to one of Dan's mates' houses.' She rested her chin on her hands. 'Sometimes I wish we could do something else for a change. It's so boring living in a village.'

Just then Tom came downstairs. 'Is Dad around?'

'He's talking to the producer,' I said. 'He should be back in a minute.'

'Great,' Tom said. 'I need him to take me to a band practice.'

Jessica looked up. 'Can I come with you?'

'Sure.' Tom shrugged.

'Brilliant. I won't be a minute,' she said, hurrying to her room.

When Jessica came down a few moments later, she had put mascara and lipstick on and changed into black trousers and a white halter-neck top. Looking at her outfit, I wondered just how much her interest in the band practice had to do with music and how much with the supposedly gorgeous lead singer, Zak.

'Tom and Dad have gone to the car,' I told her.

'See you,' she called as she ran out of the door after them.

By Saturday I had read the script through about ten times and highlighted my part with a yellow pen. I spent all afternoon learning my lines. Mum had left the night before to start her first Purr-fect for Pets job, looking after two cavalier King Charles spaniels in a village about half an hour away. She was staying there for two nights. It was strange not having her around.

'All right, who votes takeaway pizza tonight?' Dad asked that evening as we gathered in the kitchen.

'Me!' we all said.

As Dad fetched the pizza menu, Jessica's mobile rang. She checked the number and walked into the lounge to take the call.

'What do you all want?' Dad asked.

'Ham and mushroom please,' I said.

'Spicy pepperoni – large,' Tom said.

'What about Jess?' Dad said.

'I'll go and ask her,' I said.

I went through to the lounge. Jessica was talking on the phone. Her voice sounded warm and flirty. 'Yeah, eight o'clock tomorrow, then,' she said. 'Me too. I'm *really* looking forward to it.' She saw me and her voice changed instantly. 'I'd better go,' she said. 'See you tomorrow. Yeah – later!'

She turned the phone off. I forgot about the pizza. 'Who was that?'

She shrugged. 'Zak,' she said casually.

'Zak!' I echoed. 'You're going out with him?'

'Not going out going out,' she said quickly. 'Just going out as friends.'

'Are you going to tell Dan?'

She looked uncomfortable. 'There's nothing for him to know about. Zak and I are just friends.'

'So why don't you tell Dan that you're seeing him, then?'

'Because he wouldn't understand,' Jess said. 'You mustn't tell him, Soph.'

As if I'd tell! I don't dob people in. 'I won't, but . . .' I was about to tell her that what she was doing wasn't right, but just then Dad came into the lounge and I quickly shut up.

'There you are,' he said. 'I thought you must have

gone upstairs. What sort of pizza do you want, Jess?'

'Tuna and sweetcorn please,' Jessica said, turning her irritation off in a flash. She went over to him. 'Do you want me to lay the table, Dad?' she asked sweetly.

'Thanks,' Dad said, looking surprised but pleased.

Jessica hurried into the kitchen, avoiding my eyes. I stared after her. I hoped my supposedly in-love, supposedly going-steady-with-her-boyfriend sister knew what she was doing.

Jessica looked really nice when she went out the next night. She was wearing a red dress that showed off her curves.

'Have fun,' Dad said as she left.

'Bye!' she replied, hurrying out of the room before I could say a word.

I found it hard to settle to anything that night. I tried to learn my lines but I just kept thinking about Jessica. She'd said she and Zak were just going out as friends, but what if it turned into something different? What would happen to her and Dan? I wanted them to stay together.

I was in bed but still awake when she came in at 11.

'Night, Dad,' I heard her say.

I jumped out of bed and opened my bedroom door just as she came up the stairs.

'Sophie!' she said in surprise.

'How did it go?' I demanded.

'Great.' She shrugged. 'Good night.'

She walked into her room, but I wasn't going to be put off that easily. I followed her.

'What did you do?'

For a moment I thought she was going to tell me to get out, but then her face seemed to go all soft and glowing.

'Nothing much. Just saw a film and talked.' Her eyes shone. 'Zak's amazing. He writes songs and he's into things like poetry and stuff.' She sat down and wrapped her arms round her chest. 'He told me this really good poem about a gazelle and said it reminded him of me.'

'Did you kiss him?' I asked, looking at her dreamy face in alarm.

Relief washed over me as Jessica shook her head. 'He knows about Dan.'

'So it was just a one-off. You're not going to see him again?'

She shrugged. 'I don't know. I might.'

'Jess, you can't. What about Dan?' I said, thinking how hurt Dan would be if he found out.

She didn't answer.

'Jess!' I insisted.

'I'm going to bed,' she said, getting up without answering my question. 'Night, little sister.' She turned me round and started propelling me towards the door.

'All right, I'm going,' I said, shaking her hand off my shoulder.

I went back to my room and climbed into bed, feeling worried. Just what was Jessica getting herself into?

Over the next few weeks, Jessica saw Zak several times. She didn't tell me, but she didn't have to. It was obvious. She always got herself really dressed up when she saw him and hurried out of the house really quickly. Still, I didn't have much time to worry about it. My life was totally busy. There were all my lines to learn and a whole load of end-of-term stuff was happening at school – the leavers' disco, the school play, induction days at Charles Hope and, of course, the summer fair.

Tom's band played and, miracle of miracles, Ally was right, it was actually quite cool that he was my brother. Justine Wilcox even asked me to get his autograph for her! Then, almost before I knew it, it was the last day of term and everyone was packing up their things and promising to be friends forever.

'I can't believe we won't be coming back here,' I said to Ally and Harriet as we walked out of school for the last time that afternoon.

'I know,' Harriet said. 'What do you think it's going to be like at Charles Hope?'

'Scary,' I replied.

'I'm sure I'm going to get lost,' Harriet agreed. 'And –'

'I can't believe you two are talking about school!' Ally interrupted. 'It's the start of the summer holidays!

We should be talking about fun things!' She linked arms with us and declared, 'This is going to be the best summer holiday ever!'

I nodded and took a deep breath. Ally was right — it was!

Chapter Eight

'Is this where the read-through's going to be?' I asked Mum as we drove into the car park of a large country-house hotel the very next day.

She nodded.

'It's really posh,' I said, looking at the tall, imposing building. It was made of grey stone and had turrets almost like a castle.

'The actors who don't live locally are all staying here during the filming,' Mum explained.

She parked. As we walked up the smart stone steps to the entrance, I felt suddenly nervous. This was it. I was about to meet everyone else in the film. What if they didn't like me?

The receptionist behind the front desk smiled at us. 'Good morning. Can I help you?'

'We're looking for the Durrell Room,' Mum said. 'We're here for the film read-through.'

'I'll show you where to go,' the woman said, coming round the desk. We followed her down a long, red-carpeted corridor. My palms felt sweaty. What if I messed up my lines? A vision of a roomful of people laughing at me filled my mind.

'Here we are,' the receptionist said, pushing open a grand wooden door to reveal a large room with big bow windows. There were lots of people milling round and for a moment I just wanted to turn and run back to the car.

But then, to my relief, I saw a familiar face coming towards us. It was Cathy from the auditions.

'Sophie, Mrs Tennison,' she said warmly, 'do come in.'

We left the receptionist and walked into the room. 'There's tea, coffee and juice over there.' Cathy pointed to a table in one corner with several huge silver flasks of tea and coffee and jugs of orange juice on it. 'Help yourselves to whatever you want. We'll be starting the read-through in about ten minutes.' She looked round. 'Ah, there's Ismene Brooks and her mum.' She motioned to the window, where a woman and a girl about my age were standing. 'I must introduce you. Issy's playing the part of Becky.'

I looked at the girl. She was wearing black jeans, high-heeled shoes and a black strappy top. Her shiny strawberry-blonde hair fell to her shoulders, sleek and straight. She looked very glamorous and grown up, and also kind of familiar.

She looked up curiously as Mum and I walked over with Cathy. I had the strange feeling that I had seen her somewhere before.

'Issy, this is Sophie Tennison,' Cathy said. 'She's playing Sara.'

Issy smiled. 'Hi.'

Cathy glanced round as some more people came in. 'I'd better go,' she said. 'I'll leave you all to introduce yourselves properly.'

She hurried off.

Mum introduced herself to Issy's mother. 'Annie Tennison.'

'Caroline Brooks,' Issy's mum replied, holding out her hand. She was very elegant-looking, with the same thick strawberry-blonde hair as her daughter, only hers was cut in a short shining bob.

'Caroline Brooks,' Mum said, frowning slightly. 'Are you the newsreader?'

'Yes, on the ten o'clock news,' Mrs Brooks said with a smile.

Wow! I stared at her. I'd never met a proper famous person before.

Suddenly I realized Issy was looking at me. 'How many films have you done before?' she asked. Her green eyes were curious.

'None,' I replied. 'How about you?'

'It's my fourth.' Issy said it casually, as if it was no big deal.

'Issy's always in one thing or another,' Mrs Brooks put in. 'She goes to Hampton Academy of Performing

Arts. She's in *The Fortune Hunters* on children's BBC at the moment.'

The Fortune Hunters! It was one of my favourite programmes. Suddenly I realized why she looked so familiar.

'You're Alice!' I gasped.

Issy nodded.

'But I love *The Fortune Hunters*,' I blurted out. 'I watch it every week. It's brilliant and I think you're really good.'

As the words babbled out of me, I suddenly realized what I was saying and my cheeks blazed. How uncool could you get? Issy was bound to think I was just sucking up because she was in a TV show.

However, she didn't seem to mind. She smiled in a really friendly way. 'Thanks,' she said. She looked round. 'Look, do you want to get a drink? I'd like another orange juice.'

I glanced at Mum, who nodded.

We went over to the drinks table. At least five people said hello to Issy on the way and one woman hugged her.

'You seem to know everyone!' I said enviously.

Issy shrugged. 'They're just people I've worked with before.' She looked at me curiously. 'So, how did you get the part of Sara?'

I hesitated. What if she looked down on me because I didn't go to drama school? I realized she was looking at me expectantly. Taking a deep breath, I told her all about it.

Issy's eyes widened as she listened. 'That's so cool!' she exclaimed as soon as I'd finished. 'Half of the girls in my school auditioned for the part. You must be really good! That's just amazing!'

I felt a warm glow rush through me. It was OK! She sounded really impressed.

She grinned at me. 'You know, I think we're going to have fun doing this film!'

Feeling suddenly happy, I poured a glass of orange juice. 'So, who do you know in the cast?' I asked.

'Well, over there there's Sasha Knowles,' Issy said. 'She's playing Miss Amelia. I know her.' The actress she was pointing to was wearing a white trouser suit and had long shiny dark hair. I recognized her from a TV sitcom, *Mad House*. She was also always in the papers.

'How do you know her?' I asked.

'I did an episode of *Mad House* a year ago.' Issy shrugged.

She was so cool! She was talking about being in all these TV programmes and things as if it was just a normal part of life.

'Who's the woman she's talking to?' I asked eagerly. 'Is she an actress?'

The woman was very striking-looking. She was about fifty and had reddy-grey hair tied back in a bun.

'Yes. She's called Gillian Grace and she's playing

Miss Minchin in the film,' Issy replied. 'She's done some theatre stuff I think,' she said vaguely. 'But not much telly or film. She's not really that famous –' She broke off suddenly. 'Oh, look. There's Georgina Morrell.'

I followed her gaze. A girl was coming into the room. She looked about twelve and had a round face and big blue eyes. Her pale-blonde hair was tied back in a single plait and she was wearing trainers, tight blue jeans and a red football shirt.

'I did a TV show with her last year,' Issy told me. 'She's playing Ermyngarde in the film.'

Georgina saw us and headed over.

'Issy! Hi!' she exclaimed, looking delighted.

I smiled a greeting but she totally ignored me.

'How *are* you?' she said, looking at Issy. 'It's been ages since you e-mailed me last.'

'You know what it's like,' Issy said quickly. She turned to introduce me. 'Georgina, this is Sophie. She's Sara.'

'Oh, hi,' Georgina said, turning to look at me.

'It's an amazing story how she got the part,' Issy went on excitedly. 'She doesn't even go to a performing arts school. She –'

'I was so glad when I heard you were going to be Becky,' Georgina said, interrupting her. She linked her arm through Issy's and turned her back slightly to me. 'It's going to be brilliant working together again, isn't it? It'll be just like last year.'

Disappointment stabbed through me as I stood to one side, feeling like a spare part. I know I'd only met Issy five minutes ago, but I'd been hoping that we might be friends. However, Georgina was making it very clear that Issy was her friend and that she didn't want me trying to tag along.

'So, have you spoken to Lucy or Danny?' she was saying to Issy. 'I went to Tiff's party last month . . .'

I shuffled awkwardly on the spot and wondered if anyone else would come and talk to me. There were some older girls and one who looked a lot younger, maybe about eight. But the only people my age were Issy and Georgina. My heart sank.

Bill clapped his hands. 'All right, everyone. If you'd like to come and take a seat at the table with your scripts and we'll get started.'

At last! A chance to escape. I hurried thankfully back to Mum.

'Here's your script,' Mum said. 'I've just spoken to Cathy. She says there's no need for me to stay while you do the read-through, so I'm going to go and have a coffee outside with Caroline. You don't mind, do you? I'm sure you'll concentrate better if I'm not here.'

I swallowed. I'd have liked to ask her to stay, but I didn't want to seem babyish. 'That . . . that's fine,' I muttered.

'Go and sit down, then,' Mum encouraged me.

I looked at the big table. People were sitting down

and getting out bottles of water, pens and scripts. Where was I going to sit?

Just then, Issy hurried up to me. 'There you are! Why did you disappear like that? Come on. Let's sit together. There are two seats over there by Sasha.'

I looked at her in surprise. 'What about Georgina?' I could see the blonde girl already sitting at the table with an empty seat beside her. 'Aren't you going to sit with her?'

'No. Why should I?' Issy looked confused. 'Don't you want to sit by me?'

'Yeah, but . . . well, I thought you two were friends,' I said.

'We are, sort of,' Issy replied. 'But not like best friends.' She lowered her voice. 'Georgina's OK, but she can be really annoying at times and she's got no idea about clothes. Just look at what she's wearing! I mean, a football shirt and tight jeans! Pur-lease!'

She linked arms with me and we went over to the table together. As we approached, Georgina frantically patted the chair beside her, but Issy just shrugged and smiled and sat down next to Sasha Knowles.

'Hi,' she said to the glamorous actress. 'Do you remember me? I did an episode of *Mad House* with you last year.'

I watched in amazement as she chatted away. I'd never met anyone this confident. She was so bright and lively. She just seemed to assume that people would like her – and they did. Sasha was soon laughing with her and chatting back.

I looked across the table at Georgina. She seemed very fed up. I tried to smile at her, but she just scowled and looked away.

At last everyone was sitting down and Bill held up his hand. 'OK, guys. Quiet please! I think what we'll do first is go round the table and introduce ourselves. I'll start. I'm Bill Armstrong and I'm the producer.'

Laurence was sitting next to him, his long hair pulled back in a ponytail. A baseball cap was on the table beside his script. 'I'm Laurence and I'm the director.'

I waited nervously for my turn. Sasha Knowles spoke and then Issy and then everyone turned to look at me. I swallowed, feeling my cheeks go red. 'I'm Sophie Tennison,' I announced, trying as hard as I could not to sound nervous. 'And I'm playing Sara.'

I saw people's faces register interest but, to my relief, before I had time to feel embarrassed, the man sitting next to me spoke.

'I'm Alan Thomas and I'm playing Mr Crewe, Sara's father.'

He winked at me. I smiled back. He seemed nice.

After everyone had said their names, the read-through started. Laurence read out the directions at the top of each page and then people took it in turns to say their lines. I was nervous to begin with, but by the time I had reached the end of my first scene I felt OK. One scene flowed into another and soon I hardly noticed the time passing.

'Great!' Laurence said, when we reached the end. 'That will do for today. I'll see you at rehearsals and on the set.'

Everyone stood up.

'So, what did you think of your first read-through?' Issy said as we picked up our scripts and the call sheets that told us when we were needed over the next few days. 'I hope you can remember everyone's names,' she teased.

'I can remember about two of them,' I admitted.

Just then Georgina came over. Ignoring me, she turned to Issy. 'Why didn't you sit with me, Is?' she said, looking hurt.

Issy just shrugged. 'I wanted to sit over here with Sophie.'

Just then our mums came back into the room.

'Anyway, got to go,' she said quickly. 'See you at rehearsal, Georgina!' She hurried off.

I hesitated. Georgina was looking quite upset. I felt a bit bad. Maybe I should try to be friendly.

'Well, I'll . . . er . . . I'll see you tomorrow,' I said.

Georgina shrugged coldly. 'Whatever.' She walked away.

So much for trying to be friends! I frowned at her rudeness. Like it was my fault that Issy had chosen to hang round with me!

I had gone to join Issy by our mums when Bill came over. 'Sophie, would you come for a quick costume fitting before you leave, please?'

I nodded.

'I'll see you at rehearsal, then,' Issy said. 'I'm not needed tomorrow, but I'll be there on Monday.'

'OK, I'll see you then,' I replied.

We said goodbye and Issy went off with her mum. While Mum waited, I followed Bill into a smaller room where a load of costumes were hanging on rails.

There was a lady there. She smiled. 'Hi, I'm Liz, the wardrobe supervisor. I've got some costumes for you to try on.'

When Liz had finished with me, I went back to Mum, who was now talking to Gillian Grace.

'All done?' Mum asked as I hurried over.

I nodded.

Mum smiled at Gillian. 'Well, it was lovely to meet you, Gillian. Like I say, I really am a huge fan.'

Gillian smiled at her. 'You're too kind.' She turned her large hazel eyes on me. 'I'll see you tomorrow for our rehearsal, Sophie. I thought you did very well at the read-through. They're always nerve-racking occasions.'

'I was a bit nervous,' I admitted. 'At first anyway.'

'You couldn't tell,' Gillian said reassuringly. 'Are you looking forward to rehearsals starting?'

'I am.'

'Well, if you're unsure about anything, just ask me,' Gillian said, smiling at me warmly.

'Thank you,' I said, liking her.

Mum and I said goodbye to her and made our way to the car.

'Goodness, I can't believe I've just met Gillian Grace,' Mum said, looking quite starry-eyed. 'Wasn't she nice?'

I nodded.

'She's played all the classic roles for women in the theatre,' Mum said. 'She's a simply wonderful actress.'

I frowned. 'Issy said she isn't that famous.'

'Really?' Mum looked surprised. 'Well, I suppose she's not famous in the sense that she usually does plays in the theatre rather than films or TV things and she hardly ever gives interviews. But she's one of our greatest stage actresses.'

I pictured Gillian Grace in my mind. She was tall and striking, but she didn't look like I'd imagined a great actress would. She'd been wearing dull brown trousers and a green shirt. She hadn't even had any make-up on.

'You're very lucky to have the chance to act with her,' Mum said. 'And with all the other actors and actresses involved. This film is going to be an amazing experience for you.'

I agreed. I couldn't wait!

*

As soon as I got home, I rang Harriet. Her dad told me she was at Ally's house, so I rang there.

Ally picked up the phone. 'Sophie!' she exclaimed when she heard my voice. 'Harriet!' she shouted. 'It's Sophie! Come here!' She spoke to me again. 'So how was the read-through? What was it like?'

'Brilliant,' I said.

'Did you meet anyone famous?' Ally asked.

'Lots of people. There was Sasha Knowles and then this girl, Issy. She's Alice in *The Fortune Hunters*. She's really nice and . . .'

'What's she saying?' I heard Harriet ask in the background. 'We've been thinking about you all day, Soph!' she called.

'Why don't you come over?' Ally said to me. 'Mum's said we can have a sleepover. We can talk properly then.'

'OK. I'll just ask,' I said. I turned. Mum was tidying up around the sofa. 'Mum, Ally's having a sleepover tonight. Can I go?'

To my astonishment, Mum shook her head.

'Why not?' I demanded.

'I'm sorry, love, but I really don't think it's wise,' Mum said. 'Not while you're working. You have to be at rehearsals at nine tomorrow morning – you'll be far too tired if you've been up half the night talking.' She saw my face. 'Look, maybe next weekend. You've got Sunday off, so it won't matter if you're tired then.'

'But that's a whole week away!' I protested. 'You mean I can't sleep over in the week at all, even though it's the holidays?'

'Not while you're working on the film,' Mum said.

I stared at her in frustration, but I could tell from the tone of her voice that there was no point arguing. 'I can't come,' I said to Ally.

'I heard,' she said.

'What's up?' Harriet asked.

'Sophie's mum won't let her come,' Ally replied.

Harriet took the phone. 'That's awful.'

'I know,' I said. I felt all sort of hollow inside. I hated the thought of the two of them staying at Ally's without me.

'We could cancel it,' Harriet suggested.

Part of me wanted to say yes, but I knew that would be mean. 'No, no, you stay,' I heard myself saying.

'Are you sure?' Harriet asked worriedly.

'Yeah, sure,' I replied.

'It won't be nearly as good without you,' Harriet said.

'Look, I've got to go,' I said quickly. The sympathy in her voice was making me feel like crying. 'Have a good time.'

I put the phone down and Mum came over to me. 'I'm sorry, love,' she said. 'Look, tell you what. Why don't you invite them over for a sleepover here next Saturday? We'll make it a special night. You can have whatever food you like and I'll take you all to the video shop.'

'OK,' I said, but although it was nice of Mum, it didn't change that fact that Ally and Harriet were going to be staying together tonight.

Mum smiled. 'That's settled, then. Now, can I get you a drink or a snack before supper?'

I shook my head. 'I'm going to my room.'

I walked slowly up the stairs. All the excitement I had been feeling after the read-through had gone flat. Maybe doing this film wasn't so wonderful after all . . .

I stopped the thought right there. Was I mad? Of course doing the film was wonderful. It was the best thing that had ever happened to me. It was like having a dream come true.

Wasn't it?

Chapter Nine

'Good, good! Yes, that's it! It's getting there!' Laurence said. He was sitting behind a desk, watching intently as Alan and I rehearsed our first scene together.

We had only been rehearsing for half an hour but the first pages of my script were already covered in instructions saying things like 'move to the right', 'look out of the window' and 'act v. sad'. The way it worked was Laurence spoke to us about what he wanted us to do in the scene and then we went through it until he was happy. Alan had told me to write everything down so that I remembered it when we started actually filming the scenes.

'Great,' Laurence said as Alan and I ran through the scene for the fifth time. 'That worked well. Remember that.' He glanced round at Steve, who was sitting beside him. 'We'll do scene four now.'

Steve stood up. 'Scene four, everyone, please!' he called.

'We're not in this scene, so take a break now,' Alan said to me. 'But stay in the room in case you're needed.'

'Thanks,' I said gratefully.

He seemed to be going out of his way to make sure that I knew what to do. But then so was everyone. All the cast and crew were being really friendly.

Taking my script, I went over and sat by Mum.

At lunch time, I saw Issy walking across the hotel lawn with her mum.

Issy's face broke into a grin when she saw me. 'Sophie! How are rehearsals going?'

'Great,' I said.

'Do you want to come and see my room?' she asked eagerly. 'It's really big.'

'I'll just go and ask,' I said.

I ran back to Mum, who was sitting on a wooden bench in the shade.

'OK,' she said when I told her what I wanted. 'But remember that rehearsals start again at two.'

I nodded and went upstairs with Issy.

Her room *was* huge. It had a big window that looked over the garden, a television and a separate bathroom. There were hair and make-up things all over the desk and Issy had put up some photographs. There were lots of her and her friends in pantomimes and shows.

'Going to stage school must be cool,' I said. 'Do you learn all about acting and stuff?'

'Yeah, we do acting, dancing and singing classes.'

'Instead of real lessons?' I asked.

'No. We still have to do maths and things, worse

luck,' Issy replied. 'We just do the other classes as well.'

I sighed enviously. 'I'd love to go. Does . . . does Georgina go to stage school too?'

Issy nodded. 'She's been acting since she was really little.' She grinned. 'Something she'll remind you of over and over again.'

'What do you mean?' I asked.

'Oh, she's always going on about the things she's been in.' Issy went to her desk and started to put on some silvery-white eyeshadow. 'Just you wait. She'll be telling you all about it soon.'

'Do you really not like her, then?' I asked curiously.

Issy shrugged. 'She's OK, I guess. I mean, I don't hate her or anything, but she can be a bit weird.' She flashed a smile at me from the mirror. 'I like you more.'

I felt delighted.

'So, what's your school like?' Issy said, picking up her mascara.

'Just normal. It's not very big, but I like it. Well, I did,' I said, remembering. 'I'm not going there any more. I'll be starting secondary school in the autumn.'

'Me too,' Issy said. 'But at my school it's still part of the same school. It's just called the senior department.' She looked at me earnestly. 'Are you worried about starting at a new school?'

'A bit,' I admitted. 'We had an induction day and it was all right. It was just really big. I'm sure I'm going to get lost or something. It seems ages away, though. I mean, there's all the filming first.'

I watched as Issy applied mascara. She looked so confident. If I ever use mascara I usually end up with big black blobs under my eyelashes.

'You've got loads of make-up,' I said, looking enviously at all the pots.

'This colour would suit you,' she said, picking up a pot of pale-pink lip-gloss. 'Try it.'

I reached out with my finger, but Issy pulled the pot away.

'No, you have to use a brush, otherwise it'll smudge round your mouth,' she said. 'Look, like this.'

She picked up a lip brush and, dipping it into the little pot, she carefully filled in her lips.

'You try now,' she instructed, handing me another brush.

I copied her.

'It looks good,' she said, smiling as I finished.

I smiled back at her. She was so cool. She seemed to know about everything!

After I'd put the lip-gloss on, I sat on her bed and we talked and talked. I was enjoying myself so much that I almost forgot to go back to rehearsals, but Issy's mum knocked on the door to remind me.

Saying goodbye, I ran down the stairs and raced along the corridor to the rehearsal room. Luckily I got there just before 2 o'clock.

Georgina was already in the rehearsal room. Her white-blonde hair was tied back in a long plait and she wearing a dark-blue tracksuit.

I paused. OK, Issy had said she was a bit strange and she hadn't been friendly the day before, but I don't like not getting on with people. Deciding to try again, I went over.

'Hi.'

Georgina hesitated and then, to my relief, smiled. 'Hi.'

I wondered what to say next. 'Umm . . . are you looking forward to rehearsals?'

Georgina nodded. 'How have they been this morning?'

'Good,' I replied.

I grinned. This was going OK. Maybe we could all be friends.

Georgina looked at me and I looked at her. Neither of us seemed to know what to say next.

I racked my brains. It's odd how with some people you feel you can talk about anything and with others you just don't seem to have anything to talk about at all. Suddenly I remembered what Issy had said about Georgina liking to talk about the parts she'd played.

'Issy said you've done quite a bit of acting before?' I said.

Georgina's face instantly lit up. 'Oh, yeah. Loads,' she said, tossing her plaits back. 'I've been in episodes of *The Bill* and *Casualty* and *Grange Hill* and I did lots of commercials when I was younger. You've probably seen them. Remember this?' she said, putting her head on one side and smiling broadly. 'Yum, yum,' she declared. 'I love the taste of Honey-coated Sugar Corn Puffs in my tum!' She stood up and burst into a little song and tap dance. 'Honey-coated Sugar Corn Puffs in my tum!' She broke off and looked at me questioningly. 'Well?'

'I . . . I think I remember,' I lied, looking round and seeing that everyone in the room was giving us surprised looks.

I edged my chair away slightly. OK, Issy was right. Georgina was definitely weird! Maybe my idea of us all being friends wasn't going to work after all.

Georgina beamed at me. 'Do you want to see the advert I did for toilet rolls?'

'Maybe later,' I gulped.

She tucked her arm through mine. 'You know Ermyngarde and Sara are best friends in the film. Well, maybe we should be best friends too.'

I smiled weakly.

To my total relief, Laurence clapped his hands. 'Back to work, guys. Scene twelve. That's Sophie and Gillian, please.'

'See you later.' Georgina smiled.

'Yeah, later,' I said, and thankfully I hurried away to join Gillian and Laurence on the set.

*

We rehearsed all afternoon. By the time Mum and I got home at 6 o'clock I felt completely exhausted.

'You look worn out,' Mum said as I sat down at the kitchen table.

'I am,' I admitted. 'There's just so much to try and remember, and I don't want to get anything wrong.'

Baxter and Wilson wagged their tails at me. Baxter pushed his black nose on to my lap and whined. I sighed. It was my turn to feed the animals.

'In a minute, Bax,' I said.

'It's OK. I'll feed them tonight,' Mum said.

'Thanks, Mum,' I said gratefully.

After supper I flopped down on the sofa and turned on the TV. Dad looked at me.

'Shouldn't you be going through your lines for tomorrow, Sophie?' he asked.

He was right.

I dragged myself off the sofa and went upstairs with my script. It was quiet because both Jessica and Tom were out. Jessica had gone to watch the band practise again, but it was obvious that was just an excuse to see Zak.

I started to read through the scenes I would be rehearsing the next day but I couldn't concentrate. I found myself thinking about Ally and Harriet. How had their sleepover been the night before? I couldn't stop thinking about it, so in the end I went to the phone and rang Harriet.

'Sophie!' she said. 'How was the rehearsal?'

'Good,' I said. 'We did loads of different scenes. How was the sleepover?'

'Brilliant! Though not as good as if you'd been there, of course,' Harriet added hastily.

'What . . . what did you do?' I asked.

'We had a barbecue,' Harriet replied, 'and made ice-cream sundaes with lemonade, Ribena and ice cream. And when we went to bed we had a pillow fight and one of the pillows burst and went everywhere. You should have seen Ally's face. We had to try and hide all the feathers under the bed so her mum didn't see them! It was really funny.'

'Yeah, it sounds it,' I managed to say.

I felt myself beginning to wish that I hadn't rung. It was really weird hearing about them having fun without me. Hadn't they missed me at all?

'We really missed you, though, Soph,' Harriet said, spookily seeming to read my thoughts. 'And we talked about next weekend. Ally said you might be allowed to sleepover then.'

'Yeah,' I said, feeling a bit more cheerful. 'In fact, Mum said you can both come here.'

'Cool!' Harriet said. 'We'll have a great time. Umm . . .' She hesitated and I could tell she had something she wanted to ask. 'You . . . you don't mind if Ally comes and stays at mine tomorrow, do you?'

Er . . . yes! I wanted to say.

'I mean, I don't want you to think we're going off together or anything. It's just we're both going riding and –'

'It's fine,' I interrupted sharply.

There was a pause.

'Sophie?' Harriet said softly.

She sounded so concerned that I immediately felt really mean for being annoyed. It wasn't her and Ally's fault that I wasn't allowed to stay over.

'Sorry,' I said. 'Look, it's fine. I really don't mind.' I tried hard to make it sound like I meant it.

'OK. Well, if you're sure,' Harriet said.

'I'm sure.' I swallowed. 'Anyway, I'd better go. I've got my lines to learn.'

'All right. Ring me tomorrow.'

'I will.'

I put the phone down and walked slowly back to my room. I looked at the script on my bed. I didn't want to sit down and learn it. I thought about Harriet. I could just see her and Ally trying to hide the feathers from Ally's mum. Was this what it was going to be like all summer? Hearing about them having fun without me?

Just then the phone rang. I went to pick it up.

'Hi, Sophie!' a familiar voice said.

'Issy!' I exclaimed in surprise.

'You don't mind me ringing you, do you? I was like totally bored with learning my lines.'

'I don't mind at all,' I said. 'I was really bored too.'

'I keep trying to watch TV,' Issy confided, 'but Mum is always coming in to check on me.' She sighed. 'I wish you were here and then we could learn them together.'

'I wish I was there too,' I said, really meaning it.

'So, how were rehearsals?' Issy asked.

I told her about Georgina's little song-and-dance routine.

Issy giggled. 'She's staying two rooms along from me. She sat by me at supper time. All she did was talk about a TV show she did a few months ago. I wish you were here instead!'

Just then Dad came upstairs. 'I need the phone, Sophie.'

'I'd better go,' I said quickly to Issy. 'I'll see you tomorrow.'

'Yeah, see ya!' Issy said.

I pressed the off button on the phone. I felt much better. Going back to my room, I picked up my script. Somehow learning my lines didn't seem nearly so bad now I knew that Issy was doing the same.

*

Chapter Ten

'Nervous?' Cathy asked as she collected me on Wednesday morning.

'A bit,' I admitted.

It felt strange to be going off without Mum, but from now on Cathy would be driving me to and from the set each day. I could hardly believe that the rehearsals were over already. But Issy had told me it was quite normal — in fact, some of the films she'd been in she hadn't had any rehearsals at all until she got on to the actual film set.

I wondered what the filming was going to be like. Putting my hand in the pocket of my shorts, I touched the tiny wooden model of a black cat that Harriet had brought round to my house the day before.

'It's for luck,' she'd said. 'I'll be thinking of you, Soph.'

That's the thing about Harriet: she always does really nice things for people.

'Thanks,' I'd replied, taking the cat and feeling touched.

'Not that you need luck.' Harriet had smiled at me. 'I bet you're going to be great.'

As Cathy drove, I stroked the cat and thought about what Harriet had said. Was I really good enough to be in a film? What if I messed up in front of the cameras? *Oh, no*, I thought, feeling suddenly scared. *Please let me do OK.*

After twenty minutes, Cathy turned the car into a long, tree-lined driveway. At the end of it stood an old red-brick school – Stanton Hall. The car-parking area in front was filled with pale-grey lorries. There were lots of people milling about. They all seemed to be wearing shorts with long T-shirts, tool belts and big boots. Most of them were carrying walkie-talkies.

Cathy parked the car and we went inside.

'Wow!' I said, looking around at the high ceilings and the portraits on the walls.

'Like it?' Cathy said.

I nodded. It was very grand. Trying to imagine what it would be like to come to school here, I followed Cathy down a wood-panelled corridor.

'This is the green room,' Cathy said, stopping by a door.

The room was light and airy, with comfy-looking chairs and a large TV.

'This is where everyone hangs out when they're not filming.'

I looked round. 'Where does the filming happen?'

'It depends,' Cathy replied. 'Today we're filming the scenes in Miss Minchin's parlour and for that we're using the teachers' common room on the first floor. Now, let's go to your dressing room. Margaret, who will be chaperoning you, should be there.'

We went up two flights of stairs to the second floor. Four large classrooms had each been split into dressing rooms with movable partitions. Cathy showed me to the one that had my name on the door.

'This is yours,' she explained. 'Someone from Wardrobe will come to help you get changed. Now, where's Margaret?'

As she spoke, a woman in her fifties came up the stairs.

'Margaret, just the person I want to see!' Cathy said. 'This is Sophie Tennison. Sophie, meet Margaret.'

Margaret smiled. 'Hello, dear.' As she smiled her eyes twinkled. She looked kind and fun.

'I'll leave you in Margaret's capable hands,' Cathy said to me. 'See you on the set later.' She hurried off.

'Come on,' Margaret said to me. 'Let's go down to Make-up. You can tell me all about yourself while you get ready.'

An hour and a half later, I stared into my dressing-room mirror. I was wearing a white dress with blue ribbons running through it and a hat that tied under my chin with more dark-blue ribbon. The dress came to just below my knees and I had white tights on and black shoes. I looked much younger than eleven but I knew that was good. When the film started I was supposed to be just seven years old.

As I turned from side to side to look at myself, I felt the stiff net petticoats of the dress rustle against my legs. 'I can't believe it's me,' I said.

'You certainly look different.'

Margaret beamed. While I'd been being made up, she had asked me all about myself and I had learned that she was assistant director Steve's mother and had been a chaperon for five years. She said she loved it. Now she glanced at her watch.

'Come on. Time to go to the set.'

As we went up the main staircase to the first floor, my heart started to bang in my chest. Since I'd arrived I'd been too busy looking round, talking to Margaret and getting ready to feel nervous, but now I began to feel worried. I was about to film the scene where Sara and her father meeting Miss Minchin for the first time. I could only vaguely remember it from the rehearsals. What if I went wrong?

We reached the landing. It was simply bustling with people. There was equipment everywhere – cameras, rolls of cable, lights on stands, trolleys. There seemed to be so much going on. I shrank close to Margaret's side.

I want to go home, I thought.

'The set's through here,' Margaret said cheerfully. 'Mind the cables on the floor.'

I followed her into one of the rooms. It was very crowded and hot. In the centre was a clear space that was brightly lit. Lights and wires surrounded it. People were hurrying about, adjusting equipment, writing notes, murmuring to each other.

Laurence was standing by the camera and talking to Gillian and Alan, who were both in costume. Looking round, he saw me. His face lit up.

'Hi, sweetheart,' he said, coming over and hugging me. 'You look just perfect!'

I felt a bit better.

'Now, come on to the set,' he said. 'We're almost ready to walk through the scene.'

I went over to where Gillian and Alan were standing.

'Hi, Sophie,' Alan said. 'All ready?'

I nodded.

Laurence pointed out a tiny piece of tape on the floor. 'When you come in with Alan, I want you to stand here on this mark,' he explained to me. 'We'll be taking quite a number of close-up shots of your face and we need you to be in the right place. Can you stand here while we take a few measurements?'

I stood on the mark. One of the men who were standing by the camera came over.

'Hi. I'm Rob, the focus-puller,' he said.

I stood as still as I could until Rob had finished taking measurements.

'OK, let's run through the scene,' Laurence said.

We had several rehearsals and then Laurence went to speak to the camera operator.

Gillian came over to me as I waited at the side of the set. 'How are you feeling?'

'Nervous,' I admitted. 'What if I get something wrong?'

'It doesn't matter,' Gillian replied. 'We'll just shoot the scene again.' She squeezed my hand. 'You'll be fine. Just relax.'

I was suddenly very glad that she and Alan were on the set for my first day.

'OK, guys,' Laurence said, coming back. 'Let's go for it.'

'Quiet on set. Starting positions please!' Steve called.

I went to stand with Alan by the door. It was hot in the room and I felt sick. *This is it,* I thought. If I go wrong now, *everyone* will see.

Laurence sat down by a trolley that had a little TV screen on it. One of the sound men crouched on the floor near the camera holding a long furry microphone that looked like a rolled-up sheepskin rug. An expectant hush fell on the room.

'Rolling!' someone called out.

Rob stepped on to the set holding a black board with white writing. 'Scene six, take one,' he said, clapping the two halves of the board together, then he moved off the set.

'And action!' Laurence called.

My stomach turned a loop-the-loop.

'Captain Crewe, please come in,' Gillian said.

I followed Alan and stopped on my mark. I swallowed, horribly aware of all the people, the camera, the lights. They seemed to be crowding in on me, but then Gillian took my hand and stroked it.

'This must be little Sara,' she said, her large hazel eyes boring into mine.

Confidence seemed to flow out of her. I stared into her eyes and suddenly everything else in the room faded away – the cameras, the lights, the people. I was Sara, seven years old, about to be separated from her beloved father, wary of this new headmistress.

'What a beautiful child,' Gillian murmured.

'She is,' Alan said fondly beside me. 'She's my little princess.'

He walked forward and hesitated. The pause grew longer. Suddenly he shook his head.

'Cut!' Laurence shouted.

I jumped in surprise. My eyes darted to Laurence in alarm. I might not know much, but I knew 'cut' meant stop filming. Was it me? Had I made a mistake?

'Sorry,' Alan said, looking embarrassed. 'First-take nerves. Line!' he called.

Phew! So it wasn't me. I took a deep breath as Gary, the second assistant director, read out the line Alan had forgotten.

'OK, places again, guys,' Laurence said.

Gillian looked at me. 'See,' she said softly, 'if something goes wrong, we just do it again.'

As the crew reset, Laurence came over.

'That was perfect, Sophie. I loved the way you looked so nervous and yet excited at the same time. Can you keep that expression for me? It was just right.'

I swallowed a grin and nodded. If only he knew!

We went back to our starting positions and five minutes later we were ready to try again.

'Scene six, take two!' Rob announced.

It took nineteen takes before Laurence called, 'Cut! That's a wrap!'

'That means we're finished,' Alan told me.

I stretched, feeling very relieved. I'd been beginning to think we were never going to finish the scene! There had always seemed to be some reason why we had to do another take – either someone had made a mistake or Laurence had decided to film the scene from a different angle. It was really difficult, because I had to do the scene in exactly the same way every time. The only good thing was that all the waiting around between takes had bored my nerves away. So much for filming being exciting! Most of the time all you seemed to do was sit and wait. All the adults had books to read and I decided that the next day I would bring one too.

I wasn't needed for the next scene, so I went back to

the dressing rooms with Margaret. Issy was just coming out of the one next to mine.

'Issy!' I exclaimed in delight. 'Hi!'

She grinned. 'Look at you!'

'Should I wear it to the school disco?' I said, giving a twirl.

'Umm – maybe not,' Issy replied with a smile.

'Is that your dressing room?' I asked her.

'Yes,' she said. 'We'll have to bring posters in and decorate them.'

I saw a grey-haired woman talking to Margaret. 'Who's that?'

'Joan, she's the other chaperon,' Issy said. 'She's really nice. She's bought a load of craft stuff that we can use and Cluedo and Mouse Trap for us to play.'

'Issy, time to go to Wardrobe,' Joan said.

I wanted to go with them, but Margaret said I should have lunch. We went to the school dining hall, where caterers were serving food. A lot of it sounded strange – Galician meatballs, stir-fried pork with chillies and ginger, sauté potatoes. I ended up just having ham and salad and some fried potatoes that were sort of like little square chips.

Afterwards I went to the green room with Margaret. At 2.30 Issy came to find me there and we messed about for a bit, drawing pictures to decorate our dressing rooms, and then we went back to the set to do a scene together.

It was just like in the morning – rehearsing, having measurements taken, waiting about while things were moved about, filming a scene and then filming it again and again. Only this time I had Issy to talk to, which made it much more fun.

'Is there always so much waiting around when you do a film?' I asked her as we stood at the side of the set between takes.

'Always,' she replied. 'It won't be so bad next week when all the extras are here and we do the big school-room scenes. We'll probably be really busy then. There'll be more rehearsals and we'll be on set most of the time.' She looked at me in surprise. 'Why? You're not bored, are you?'

'No way,' I said quickly. 'I love filming.'

Issy smiled. 'Me too.'

'That was good,' Issy said on Friday as we walked back to the dressing rooms after finishing a scene together.

'Only six takes,' I agreed, feeling proud of myself for using the right words.

All the words that had meant nothing to me on the first day, like *boom* and *take* and *rolling*, were slowly starting to make sense now. Soon, I hoped, I would be using them as easily as Issy did.

We went up to our dressing rooms and got out of our costumes.

'What are you doing at the weekend?' I asked Issy.

Although I was filming on Saturday, I knew she had both Saturday and Sunday off.

'Going back to London,' she said. 'Mum's coming for me tonight. I think I'll go shopping with her and maybe catch up with some of my friends. Sapphire, one of my best friends, has just finished filming for the latest series of *Hollyoaks*, so I want to see her. I'd also like to catch the new Brad Pitt movie. It's opening in Leicester Square this weekend. I might ask Mum if she can get tickets to it.'

I felt a flicker of jealousy. Issy's life sounded so glamorous – meeting up with famous friends, shopping in London, going to see movies the day they opened. But then I thought about my sleepover with Ally and Harriet on Saturday night and my jealousy faded. It was a whole week since I'd seen them properly and I was beginning to have serious withdrawal symptoms! Talking on the phone just wasn't the same.

'What about you? What are you doing?' Issy asked me.

'Having a sleepover with Ally and Harriet,' I said.

'Sounds fun,' Issy said.

I nodded. Mum had said we could have a Chinese takeaway and we had also all arranged to get loads of sweets and crisps for a midnight feast. Oh, yes, Saturday night was going to be lots of fun!

*

'Let's do our nails now,' I said.

'Bagsy mine first!' Ally said.

'OK, Harriet and I'll do them together,' I said.

We were in my bedroom experimenting with a nail-painting kit that Mum had bought me. I think she'd been feeling guilty about banning me from sleepovers in the week and it was her way of making up. It had four different bottles of nail varnish and a packet of tiny nail transfers.

'I want the gold nail varnish on,' Ally said, inspecting the colours.

'You should see the make-up artists on the film set,' I said as I started to paint gold nail varnish carefully on to Ally's thumbnail. 'They're called Jules and Sandy and they're brilliant. Yesterday afternoon, when Issy and I weren't filming, they showed us how to do fake scars and things. Issy did this amazing cut on her hand. When Margaret saw it she almost died.' I grinned as I remembered Margaret's face. 'She was really worried and –'

'Who's Margaret?' Harriet interrupted.

'She's one of the chaperons,' I said. 'She's Steve's mum.'

'Steve?' Ally said, frowning.

'You know, the first AD.'

'AD . . .' Now Harriet was frowning. 'That means . . . yes, I know, assistant director,' she said, looking pleased with herself.

I nodded. I'd told them that about ten times!

'Steve was the one who auditioned you, wasn't he?' Harriet checked.

'No, that's Gary,' Ally said.

'No, Gary's the second AD,' I told her. 'Harriet's right. Steve did the auditions – with Cathy.'

'Who's Cathy?' Ally said.

She and Harriet both looked totally confused. I felt a wave of frustration. I wanted to talk about everything that was happening on the set, but they just couldn't seem to remember who the people were or what they did. I'd told them both about a million times!

'Cathy's one of the third ADs. Oh, it doesn't matter,' I said almost crossly.

There was a moment's awkward silence.

Harriet cleared her throat and quickly changed the subject. 'So . . . er . . . where's Jessica tonight?'

'Out at a party.'

I tried to stop feeling cross. It wasn't their fault they didn't know who was who on set.

'With Zak or Dan?' Ally asked.

'Zak,' I said. 'Although, I don't think they are there together together. He's playing in the band and she's gone along too.'

'Does Dan know about Zak?' Ally asked me.

I shook my head.

'I bet he'd freak if he did,' Harriet said. 'There,' she added, finishing Ally's last nail. 'All done. What do you think?'

Ally held up her fingers. 'They look cool! I think I'll get some gold nail varnish when we go into town on Monday.'

I looked at them in surprise. 'You're going into town on Monday?'

Harriet nodded. 'Dad's dropping us off in the morning and collecting us later.'

'We're going to look round all the shops,' Ally said. 'There's this new jewellery shop near the statue. It's got loads of different beads and you can buy stuff to make your own necklaces and bracelets. We're definitely going there, aren't we, Harriet?'

As she looked at Harriet for agreement I felt jealousy stab through me.

Harriet saw my face. 'We'd have asked you, Soph, but we knew you'd be filming all day. You don't mind, do you?'

I shook my head. I felt horribly left out, but I knew I couldn't say anything. After all, it wasn't their fault I wasn't around to go with them.

'Are you filming all next week?' Ally asked.

'Yeah,' I said, with an effort. 'We're doing all the big schoolroom scenes, so there'll be loads more people. All the extras are coming.'

'Will Justine be there?' Harriet asked.

I nodded.

'Lucky you – *not*!' Ally said.

We exchanged smiles and, for a while, everything

felt just about normal again. But when we went to bed that night – Ally and Harriet sleeping on camp beds on my floor, as they always did when they slept over – I couldn't get to sleep. I kept thinking about them going into town together. I knew it was dumb, but I just wished they'd asked me.

I turned over restlessly. Ally, Harriet and I had always done everything together, but suddenly all that had changed. Now it felt like I was going in one direction and they were going in another.

But I don't want to go in a different direction from them, I thought anxiously. *I want things to stay just the same as they've always been.*

✦

Chapter Eleven

I was still awake when Jessica came in.

'Night, Dad,' I heard her mutter as she climbed the stairs.

I got out of bed and tiptoed round Ally and Harriet. Had Jess had a good time at the party?

Creeping out of my door, I stopped in shock. Jessica's face was damp with tears.

'Jess?' I said quickly. 'What's the matter?'

'Nothing,' she said abruptly.

'Yeah – it looks like it!'

She opened her bedroom door.

I followed her. 'What's happened? What's wrong?'

For a moment I thought she was going to tell me to mind my own business, but then she sat down on her bed and rubbed a hand over her eyes. 'It's Zak. He . . . he acted like I didn't exist. Just because he was in the band, all these girls hung round him and he hardly even looked at me.'

I frowned. 'So? You're not going out with him.'

'I know, but . . .' Jessica broke off. 'Oh, what's the point. You won't understand.'

I felt hurt. 'I will.'

Jessica hesitated. 'It's just . . . well, I thought we were friends, Soph, that I meant something to him, and then tonight, when these other girls were there, he was really different. He even kissed some of them.' She laughed bitterly. 'Three of them in fact.'

'What did you do?' I said, my eyes widening.

'I ignored him,' she said, shrugging. 'Arrogant moron.'

I frowned. Zak sounded like he had been awful, but then I couldn't help thinking that Jessica was being unreasonable. After all, she wasn't going out with Zak, was she? Why shouldn't he kiss other girls? However, something told me that wasn't what Jessica wanted to hear.

'He's horrid,' I declared.

Jessica swallowed. 'You're right.' She took a deep breath. 'And from now on, he can jump off a tall building for all I care. I don't want anything more to do with him. I'm going to stick with Dan.'

I felt like hugging her. 'Dan's much nicer anyway,' I told her.

Jessica's forehead furrowed. 'You haven't even met Zak.'

I shrugged. 'It doesn't matter. I still know Dan's much nicer.'

'You know something —' Jessica managed a weak smile — 'I think you're right.'

*

'So what shall we do today?' I asked Ally and Harriet the next morning.

To my surprise, they exchanged glances over the box of Frosties. 'Well, actually,' Ally said, rather awkwardly, 'there's a demonstration on at the stables. It's all about Western riding and me and Harriet said we'd go.'

I stared. They were going to spend the day without me!

'You could come too, Sophie,' Harriet said quickly.

I tried to hide the hurt I was feeling. 'Yeah, and spend the rest of the day sneezing,' I said, making my voice sound light and jokey. 'You know what my hay fever's like.'

My jokiness didn't fool Harriet. 'Maybe I won't go,' she said quickly.

'You've got to, Harriet!' Ally protested. 'We've got tickets and we said we'd help put the bales of straw out for everyone to sit on!'

'But —'

'It's OK,' I interrupted Harriet. 'You go. I've got lines to learn anyway.'

'Well, if you're sure,' she said, looking at me anxiously.

I summoned all my acting powers and smiled. 'Sure,' I told her.

After breakfast, they got their things together.

I waved them off and then mooched around the house. I was soon feeling very bored. There was nothing to do and no one to talk to. Mum had stayed the night at a client's house, looking after a miniature horse and two dogs. Tom was in bed. Dad was out cycling and as soon as Jessica was up she got dressed and went round to see Dan.

I watched some TV for a bit and then picked up my script. I stared at the words, but they wouldn't seem to go into my head. I kept thinking about Ally and Harriet. They were probably in Ally's dad's car now, on the way to the riding stables. They'd be talking and laughing. And tomorrow they'd be going into town together and having even more fun. I felt a wave of loneliness and self-pity. It wasn't fair.

Don't be so selfish, I thought quickly. What do you expect them to do? Hang around at home moping just because you're busy for the holidays? If you were a proper friend you'd be glad they're having a good time. I mean, you've got the film and Issy and everything. It's not like you're missing out.

No, but I want them to miss me a bit . . .

The second the thought entered my mind I stopped it. Feeling like a very horrid, mean person, I tried hard to feel happy that Ally and Harriet were having fun.

It worked – well, almost.

'Sophie – hi!' Issy cried when I went up to the dressing rooms the next day with Cathy. She hugged me. 'I've really missed you!'

I smiled at her enthusiasm. 'It's only been two days.'

'It seems like forever.' Issy linked arms with me. 'So, come on, how was your weekend?' Before I could reply she went on, 'I had *the* best time. Do you like this?' She pointed to the short green skirt she was wearing. 'I bought it in this really cool little shop on the King's Road. It was mega-expensive.'

'It's lovely,' I said enviously.

'I just had to buy it. My friend Sapphire bought a blue one. We shopped all day Saturday and then we went out in the evening to this Italian restaurant. We went with her parents, but they let us sit on our own at another table and the waiter flirted with us all evening!' She sighed happily and then looked at me. 'How was your sleepover?'

'OK.' I shrugged.

'Just OK?' she said.

'It was fun,' I said. I paused and then decided to tell her what was worrying me. 'It was just that it was . . . different from normal.'

'How?'

I struggled to explain. 'Well, Ally and Harriet have been doing all this stuff together.'

Issy looked confused. 'So?'

I began to feel silly. 'It just felt weird.' I could see from Issy's expression that she didn't understand. 'We normally do everything together. It was strange hearing them talk about the things they'd been doing and the things they were planning,' I said, thinking about the shopping trip to town they were going on that day.

'Don't stress about it.' Issy shrugged. 'So what if they do stuff together. It's not like they're in a film. You're having a much better time than them.'

'That's not the . . .' I gave up. It was clear she wasn't going to understand. 'Yeah, I'm just being stupid, I guess.' I quickly changed the subject. 'So . . . um . . . have you met any of the extras yet?'

'No,' she replied. 'I saw some of them going into Make-up, but I haven't spoken to any of them yet. They're all in the green room.'

'Should we go and say hello?' I asked.

Issy hesitated. 'I suppose we could,' she said slowly.

Just then, Georgina came up the stairs. She waved. 'Hi-yi!' she said in a silly singsong voice.

Issy and I smiled briefly. Georgina always tagged along with us whenever she could. Most of the time she wasn't too bad, though I found it really irritating when she put on silly voices and pulled strange faces. She seemed to think she was being funny, but she just looked really odd. Still, Issy and I couldn't exactly avoid her when we were on the set together, so we put up with her. She made it clear she really wanted to be best friends with Issy, but that didn't bother me. I knew Issy liked me best.

'Look at me. I'm Sully from *Monsters Inc.*,' Georgina said, and she pulled a face and pretended to roar.

Issy exchanged looks with me. 'Yeah, right.' I hid my smile.

'So, what are we all going to do?' Georgina said, not seeming to notice.

Issy shrugged.

'We were about to go to the green room and meet all the others,' I said.

'Why?' Georgina said.

'What do you mean, "Why?"' I asked.

'Well, why do you want to meet them. They're just extras. Most of them haven't even got speaking parts.'

I stared at her. 'Don't be so stuck up!'

'I'm not.'

'Yes, you are.' I looked at Issy for support. But to my surprise, she didn't look as shocked by Georgina's comment as I felt.

'You don't want to go and meet them, do you, Is?' Georgina said.

'Well . . .' Issy hesitated.

'Issy!' I exclaimed.

'Yeah, OK, I'll go and meet them,' she said quickly.

Despite what she'd said, Georgina followed us downstairs. It was totally obvious she didn't want me and Issy doing things on our own. We went into the green room. There were about twenty girls there, all in costume and talking excitedly.

Joan saw us come in. 'I was wondering where you were,' she said. She clapped her hands and the chatter stopped. 'OK, everyone, I'd like you all to meet Sophie, Issy and Georgina. Sophie's playing Sara, Issy's playing Becky and Georgina's playing Ermyngarde.'

The girls stared at us. It was freaky to think that I could so easily have been one of them.

'I'm sure you'll all introduce yourselves,' Joan said, smiling at us.

She turned away and the chatter gradually started up again.

'I'm going to get a drink,' Georgina said.

'Me too,' Issy agreed. 'Coming, Soph?'

I was about to nod when I saw Justine. She was sitting by the window, looking almost nervous. That had to be a first! 'Actually I want to say hi to someone,' I said, deciding to be friendly. 'There's someone from my school over there. Are you coming with me?'

Issy hesitated. 'Come on,' I urged as Georgina walked to the fridge.

Looking almost reluctant, Issy followed me over.

'Hi, Justine,' I said.

'Sophie!' To my amazement, Justine actually smiled at me.

'How are you?' I asked.

'Fine.'

'This is Issy,' I said to her. 'Issy, this is Justine.'

Justine's eyes widened. 'You're in *The Fortune Hunters*, aren't you?'

Issy nodded.

'I watch it every week!' Justine said excitedly. 'You're brilliant!'

'Thanks,' Issy said briefly.

There was a pause. Issy glanced round. She looked distinctly bored.

Luckily, sensitivity is not Justine's strong point. She didn't seem to notice. 'Being on a film set is so cool, isn't it?' she said to me.

I nodded. 'How many days will you be filming for?'

'Ten altogether, I think, but we were told it depends on . . .'

As Justine talked, my eyes strayed to Issy. She was normally so friendly. What was up with her? A horrible thought seeped into my mind. Surely they weren't going to be all stuck up about people who just had small parts. No, I thought quickly. Georgina might be like that. But not Issy. She's much too nice.

Joan came over to me. 'Sophie, you, Issy and Georgina need to go over to Make-up now.'

I smiled at Justine. 'Well, I'll see you on the set.'

'Yeah, see you,' she said.

By lunch time we had filmed two of the schoolroom scenes. Issy had talked to everyone while we were on the set and I was beginning to think that I must have imagined her reluctance to get to know the new girls. However, as we finished lunch, she said to Georgina and me, 'Let's go up to the dressing rooms.'

'OK,' Georgina agreed as we stood up to clear our plates away.

I frowned. 'But what about the rounders match?'

It was a really sunny day and Gary had said he was going to organize a rounders match for everyone during the break.

'I don't feel like playing,' Issy said.

'But it'll be fun,' I protested.

'Boring more like,' Georgina put in. She linked arms with Issy. 'But you go if you want, Sophie.'

'No, come with us,' Issy said quickly to me.

I didn't know what to do. I wanted to join in the rounders game with everyone else, but I wanted to be with Issy as well.

'Come on, Soph,' she pleaded. 'It'll be much more fun in the dressing room. We can put on scars and things with my make-up.'

'Let's go, Issy,' Georgina said impatiently. 'She obviously doesn't want to come.'

'It's OK, I'm coming,' I said and hurried to join them.

We sat in Issy's dressing room drawing cuts and bruises on ourselves using yellow and purple eyeshadows and a red lip-liner that Issy had. It was fun, but hearing claps and cheers coming from the rounders game taking place on the lawn below, I couldn't help wondering whether I'd made a mistake. It sounded so much fun down there.

As Issy drew a cut on Georgina's leg, I went to the window and looked out. The sun was shining and everyone seemed to be playing — all the other girls, Gillian, Sasha and loads of the crew were there too. Even Laurence was joining in.

'What are you doing?' Issy asked.

'Just seeing what's going on,' I said.

'Well, it's your turn to do me now,' Issy said, holding out her arm.

I hesitated, wondering whether I should say I wanted to go outside.

Georgina looked at me hopefully, almost as if she knew what I was thinking. I didn't want to leave her and Issy together.

'Come on!' Issy told me.

I sighed, but what could I do? I didn't want to argue with her. Casting one last look out of the window, I walked over and sat down.

'Hi, Sophie. How was filming?' Jessica asked when I got home that evening. She was sitting at the table next to Dan.

'OK,' I said, flopping into a chair. 'But busy.' We hardly seemed to have stopped all afternoon.

'So, have you got any exciting gossip about the famous people in the film?' Dan asked.

I shook my head. 'Sorry.'

'Never mind,' he said.

He put his arm round the back of Jessica's chair. They looked really happy and relaxed together.

'Are you going out tonight?' I asked, glad that Jessica seemed to have got over Zak. Since the night of the party she had seemed much happier with Dan.

'No,' Jess said.

'In fact, I should be going home,' Dan said. 'I'm supposed to be cooking supper for my mum and dad tonight.'

'And you didn't invite me!' Jessica said, pretending to look offended. 'What sort of boyfriend are you?'

'The sort of boyfriend who wants to stay your boyfriend.' He grinned. 'My cooking is totally awful. I'm sure Mum's wishing she'd never suggested I should start doing a meal a week.'

'I could help you,' Jessica suggested.

'You think I'd be able to concentrate with you around,' he said softly.

Their eyes met and their heads started to move towards each other. I hastily jumped up, scraping my chair back to remind them I was there. It worked.

'Well, see you, Soph,' Dan said, getting up.

Jessica walked outside with him. I watched from the kitchen window and saw them snogging at the gate. Gross as it was, I felt a rush of relief. Things definitely seemed to be all right between them.

When Jessica came in I grinned at her. 'You like Dan again, then?'

She grinned back. 'You could say that.' She started getting the dog food out.

'So . . . so, have you spoken to Zak?' I asked, fetching the bowls for her.

Jessica shook her head. 'He keeps trying to ring me, but I haven't answered his calls since Saturday. He . . .'

Just then I heard the sound of the gate opening. I looked through the window. A boy with dark-blond hair was coming up the path. My eyes widened as I recognized his slanting eyes and dangerous smile from a photo I'd seen on Jessica's dressing table.

'Jess!' I gasped. 'It's Zak! He's here!'

Jessica looked panicked. 'I don't want to see him, Sophie!'

But it was too late. Zak had already seen us through the kitchen window. He lifted a hand in greeting and came in through the back door.

'Hey,' he said, looking at Jessica and totally ignoring me.

I stared at him. So this was the boy that all the fuss was about. OK, now I saw him for real, I could see what Jessica was going on about. He really was love-god material. But you could tell he knew it. He folded his arms and looked at her through narrowed eyes.

'What . . . what are you doing here?' Jessica stammered.

Zak shrugged. 'I just thought I'd come round and visit. You haven't been answering my calls.'

Jessica seemed to pull herself together. 'You noticed,' she said sarkily.

Zak frowned. 'You in a mood with me?'

Jessica didn't say anything.

I stepped forward. 'We're busy at the moment,' I said, hoping he'd take the hint and leave, but he didn't. He glanced at me as if I was an irritating little fly and then turned his attention back to Jessica.

'Is this cos I talked to those other girls last weekend?'

'Talking — that's a new name for it,' Jess said angrily.

A slow smile crossed Zak's face — it reminded me of the smile a crocodile might make as it approached its prey, if a crocodile could smile of course. 'Has anyone ever told you how gorgeous you look when you're angry?'

Jessica's eyes flew to his.

He stepped closer. 'You know those other girls aren't anything compared to you. They don't matter. You know you're the one I want.'

For a moment my head was filled with a bizarre image of the scene of Danny and Sandy singing 'You're the one that I want', from the movie *Grease*. Only Danny and Sandy were being played by Zak and Jessica. I shook my head to clear the picture.

'You ignored me,' Jessica said.

Ignore him now, I willed her. *Tell him to go away*. But she didn't.

'I thought we were supposed to be friends,' she said.

'We are,' Zak said. His voice dropped. 'And you know I'd like to be even closer friends if you'd let me.'

Jessica gazed into his eyes.

I stared at her in horror. What was happening here?

'Jess!' I said.

Zak threw a quick glance in my direction. 'Go away.'

I was outraged. 'You can't tell me to go away! This is my house!'

He had stopped listening. His eyes were fixed on Jessica again. 'Don't be mad at me any more, Jess,' he murmured. 'I hate it when you're mad at me.'

Jess swallowed.

I pulled at her arm. 'Let's go upstairs, Jess.'

She shook her head. 'You go. I'll be up in a minute.'

'Jess!'

But she wouldn't come. I glared at Zak, but what could I do? Short of physically pulling my sister out of there I didn't seem to have much choice. Reluctantly, I left the kitchen. Jess looked like she was almost about to forgive him. How *could* she? All that stuff about her looking gorgeous when she was angry. I mean, pur-lease! How vomitsome was that?

I heard the outside gate opening. Who was that? Hoping it would be Dad and Tom, I went to the lounge window. I stared. It was Dan! I felt a surge of alarm. What was he going to say if he walked into the kitchen and found Jessica flirting with Zak? Seeing Dan heading for the back door, I hurried back to the kitchen to warn Jessica.

'Jess!' I said, opening the door into the kitchen. 'Dan's . . .'

I stopped, my mouth falling open. Jessica and Zak were in each other's arms and they were kissing! They jumped guiltily and quickly separated. But it was too late. I saw Dan staring in through the kitchen window. He had seen the kiss too.

'Dan!' Jessica gasped.

She pulled away from Zak and ran outside. I followed her. Dan was standing stock-still.

'Dan!' Jessica said, running up to him. 'It's not what it seems. There's nothing going on . . .'

A muscle clenched in Dan's jaw. For a moment I thought he was going to storm into the house and hit Zak, but then he swung round and marched down to the gate.

'Dan!' Jessica pleaded, hurrying after him. 'Please! Listen to me!' She grabbed his arm. 'It just happened.'

Dan shook his arm free. Hurt radiated from his eyes. 'I trusted you, Jessica.'

'Dan! Please, listen . . .'

But Dan shook his head. 'I don't want to listen to anything you've got to say. We're finished.'

He opened the gate and walked off.

Jessica stared after him. 'No,' she whispered, starting to shake her head.

Zak came outside. He looked after Dan with a smirk. 'So, it's over between you guys,' he said to Jess. 'You going to go out with me, then?'

Jessica turned on him. 'Go out with you?' she cried. 'This is all your fault! Why did you kiss me, you moron?'

Zak raised his eyebrows. 'You didn't seem to mind at the time.'

I thought Jessica was going to hit him. 'Get out!' she shouted.

'So you and me –' Zak began.

'No!' Jessica said.

Zak shrugged, not looking too concerned. 'Your loss.' He opened the gate. 'See you around, babe.'

The gate clicked shut and he walked away. There was a silence. I looked at Jessica. Suddenly she turned and ran into the house.

'Jess! Wait!' I called.

I followed her into the kitchen. She sat down at the table and put her hands to her face. But I had already seen the tears.

'Jess?' I said tentatively.

'Oh, Soph,' she whispered. 'What have I done?'

I went over to her and put my arm round her. 'It'll be OK.'

'How *can* it be?' she said. 'Dan's never going to forgive me.' She rubbed her tears away. 'What have I done? I meant what I said about being over Zak and just wanting to be with Dan.'

I couldn't help myself. 'So why did you kiss him?' The words burst out of me.

'I don't know,' Jessica said. 'I guess I was flattered by all those things he was saying. It just happened. As soon as we started kissing I knew it was wrong and then you came in and . . . and . . .'

She broke off and I was sure she was thinking about Dan staring in through the window.

'Do you think Dan's ever going to forgive me?' she whispered.

'I don't know,' I faltered, remembering Dan's expression.

Jessica looked at me. 'Oh, Sophie, he's got to go back out with me. When I saw him walking off, it was the worst feeling ever.' Tears sprang to her eyes again.

She looked so miserable and unhappy, I felt awful. 'Maybe he just needs some time to calm down.'

'Yeah,' Jessica said, seizing the possibility. 'You're right. He was just really mad. I'll wait till tomorrow and talk to him then.'

The gate opened. I looked out of the window. 'It's Mum.'

Jessica jumped up. 'I'm going to my room,' she said quickly.

I went out to meet Mum.

'Hi, love. Had a good day?' Mum asked as she came to the gate, her arms loaded with grocery bags.

'Yeah,' I said. I felt in shock. I couldn't believe what had just happened.

'Can you take these?' Mum said, passing me three bags.

I carried them up to the house.

'Where's Jessica?' Mum asked, as she followed me in and dumped the rest of the shopping on the floor.

'Upstairs,' I stammered.

Mum looked at me quickly. I knew she could tell something was wrong. 'Has anything –'

'I'm just going to ring Ally,' I interrupted. 'I . . . er . . . promised I would.' I hurried out of the room before Mum could ask me any questions.

However, as I picked up the phone, I remembered that Ally and Harriet would just have got back from their shopping trip together. They were bound to want to go on about what a brilliant fun day they'd had and right now I wasn't sure I could cope with that.

I hesitated and then punched in Issy's mobile number instead.

Waiting for the phone to connect, I felt guilty. I hadn't spoken to Ally or Harriet since the morning before and they'd want to hear all about Jessica and Dan. I should be phoning them. But they would be so happy and full of their day.

The phone started to ring and I pushed the feeling of guilt down.

I'll call them tomorrow, I thought.

Chapter Twelve

It was hard to concentrate on filming the next day. I kept thinking about Jessica. Had she gone round to see Dan yet?

To make matters worse, we were filming a scene where I had lots to do. It was early on in the film where Lavinia, one of the older girls, tries to bully Sara by teasing her about how she pretends she's a princess. I had loads of lines.

'Cut!' Laurence called out as I forgot my lines for the third time.

I felt my cheeks go bright red. I hated messing up a scene. I felt rather than heard a sigh run round the rest of the cast and the crew, and my face burned even hotter.

'OK, everyone,' Gary called out to the other girls, 'let's have you back in your starting positions please.'

As people went back to their starting positions, I quickly checked over my lines.

I glanced at Issy for support, but she was busy talking to Georgina.

'Places please!' Laurence called.

I went back to my starting position, sitting in an armchair.

'And action!' Laurence called when everyone was ready.

Everything was fine until I got to my sixth line and then my mind just went blank again.

'Cut!' Laurence shouted as I broke off.

'I'm sorry,' I blurted out.

Laurence sighed. 'Take five, everyone. Then we'll go from the top again.'

As people started to move off the set, Laurence came over to me. I tensed, expecting him to tell me off, but instead he put an arm round my shoulders. 'Are you OK, sweetheart?' he asked in concern. 'It's not like you to forget your lines and lose concentration.'

'I'm fine,' I said, my face hot. 'I'm really sorry, Laurence.'

'It's OK,' he said. 'Look, take five minutes and have a read through your script.'

I nodded and headed over to the side of the room where I had left my script. It felt as if everyone was staring at me.

Sitting down, I looked desperately around for Issy. She was still with Georgina. They were laughing together and suddenly I felt very alone.

'Having trouble concentrating?'

I looked up. Gillian was standing beside me, her face kind.

'A bit,' I admitted.

She sat down beside me. 'What's wrong?' she asked softly.

'It's just stuff at home,' I said. 'I can't stop thinking about it.'

She squeezed my hand. 'I know it's hard, but you're going to have to,' she said. 'You won't be able to do the scene unless you do.' She reached for my script. 'Here, let me test you.'

As Gillian read through the scene with me, I felt the lines coming back.

'Try this exercise,' she said. 'It's a very useful one for helping you focus. Shut your eyes.' I did as she said. 'Now breathe in deeply for five seconds, hold your breath for five seconds and then breathe out for five seconds. Do it three times and as you do it think about being Sara. Go on,' she encouraged. 'Breathe in for five – one, two, three . . .'

She counted and I breathed in and thought about being Sara. Every other thought faded away and when I finally opened my eyes I felt in control again.

'Has it helped?' Gillian asked.

'Yes.' I nodded. I took another deep breath. 'Thanks, Gillian.'

'No problem.' Gillian nodded towards the set. 'I think you're needed again. Good luck.'

'Ready?' Laurence asked me as I hurried over.

'Ready,' I said. And this time I meant it. I moved into my starting position for the scene.

'And action!' Steve called.

The scene went perfectly and thirty minutes later I was heading back to the dressing rooms.

Seeing Gillian just in front of me, I hurried to catch up with her. 'Thank you for helping me,' I said gratefully. 'The breathing stuff you showed me was really useful.'

She smiled. 'I'm glad. Sometimes it can really help to have techniques like that to fall back on.'

'Do you learn stuff like that at drama school?' I asked curiously.

Gillian nodded. 'Why? Do you want to study acting?'

'When I'm older,' I said.

'That's good,' she said. 'Training properly is very important. Now,' she said, smiling, 'I'm going to get a coffee.'

As she walked off, Justine came over. I could hardly believe how different she was being on the film set. She was actually talking to me and being friendly. It was as if she was so excited about the filming that she forgot about trying to be cool. It made her much nicer.

'Sophie, there's going to be another rounders match today,' she said. 'Are you going to come and play?'

I hesitated a moment. I wanted to, but what about Issy? I remembered the way she'd been giggling with

Georgina when I'd been upset. She could have been more supportive. I made up my mind. 'Definitely,' I said to Justine.

'Great.' She smiled. 'I'll see you later, then.'

She went off to the school gym, which was doubling as the extras' dressing room, and I went upstairs to my dressing room.

Issy was there already. 'Hi,' she greeted me.

'Hi,' I replied, in a slightly reserved voice.

Issy didn't seem to notice. 'You'll never guess what,' she said, her eyes sparkling. 'Georgina told me the best gossip. She saw Jules from Make-up kissing Gary in the car park!'

'Really?' I said, my surprise making me forget my hurt feelings. 'But he's already got a girlfriend.'

'Yeah. And they were snogging properly!'

'Wow!' I said. 'So what did Georgina see?'

'We'll have to ask Jules about it,' Issy said as we got changed. 'I know! Why don't we see if she'll show us how to do tattoos at lunch time and ask her then?'

'I . . . I can't.'

'Why not?' she said, looking surprised.

'I told Justine that I'd play in the rounders game.'

'Well, just say you've changed your mind,' Issy said.

I hesitated and then shook my head. I wanted to play rounders and – I know it was probably stupid of me, but – I did still feel slightly hurt by Issy's lack of support earlier. 'I'm going to play rounders.'

I tensed, waiting for Issy to say she'd go with Georgina. But she didn't. She hesitated and then shrugged. 'OK, I guess I'll play too.'

'You will?' I said in delight.

'Yeah.' She didn't sound too thrilled, but I didn't care. I could play rounders with the others and be with Issy. I forgot all about feeling hurt. Lunch time was going to be fun!

It was. Loads of people played in the rounders game and there was a brilliant atmosphere. Even Georgina came to play when she realized that she was going to be the only one left out if she didn't.

'That was great,' I said to Issy as we went inside to get changed.

She nodded. 'Yeah – it was, wasn't it?' She sounded almost surprised.

However, as we climbed the stairs to the dressing rooms, I remembered Jessica and sighed.

'What's up?' Issy asked.

'I was just thinking about Jessica,' I told her. 'I wonder if she's rung Dan yet.'

'Well, why don't you ring her?' Issy suggested. 'You can use my mobile.'

'Really?' I said. 'Thanks!'

As soon as we got to the dressing rooms, I phoned home. Jessica answered. She didn't sound happy at all.

'I saw Dan this morning,' she said. 'He . . . he won't

go back out with me. He just kept saying he couldn't trust me any more.'

I felt awful for her. 'Maybe he'll change his mind.'

'I don't think so,' Jessica said bleakly.

When I pressed the off button, Issy looked at me. 'Well?'

I told her what Jessica had said. 'She sounds really down.'

'Poor thing.' Issy shook her head. 'It's weird. I seem to know all about her – and the rest of your family – and yet I've never met them.'

'You should come to my house one day,' I told her.

'I'd love to!' Issy exclaimed. 'It's so boring being stuck in the hotel all the time.'

'What about at the weekend?' I suggested. We were filming on Saturday morning and I knew Issy wasn't going back to London after that. 'You could stay at mine on Saturday and Mum could bring you back here the next day. You're filming Sunday night, aren't you?'

'Yeah! But I'd love to come and stay on Saturday. That's a great idea,' Issy enthused.

'OK, I'll ask,' I said.

Mum said it was fine for Issy to come and stay. I hugged her. I couldn't wait to see what Issy would make of our house – of Jessica, of Tom!

Just then the phone rang.

Mum answered it. 'It's for you, Sophie,' she said. 'It's Ally.'

Guilt jumped through me. It was almost three days since I'd rung Ally or Harriet. Usually we never went that long without speaking to each other. They'd left messages for me, but I hadn't got round to ringing them back. I took the phone from Mum feeling almost nervous. 'Hi.'

'Hello, stranger,' Ally said. 'I've tried to ring you twice – you're never in these days.'

Her voice was teasing but I could hear a slight note of hurt in it.

'Sorry,' I said, feeling bad. 'I've been really busy filming. We've been doing all the schoolroom scenes with all the extras and . . .' I stopped, realizing she wouldn't understand what the schoolroom scenes were. 'Well, it's been kind of hectic. How about you? How . . . how was town?'

'Really good,' Ally replied. 'The new jewellery shop is cool. We could go there together at the weekend.'

'I can't,' I said. 'I'm filming on Saturday morning.'

'You're filming at the weekend now as well?' Ally said, sounding dismayed.

'Just on Saturday,' I explained.

'Oh, right. So you can sleep over on Saturday night? Harriet's dad has said we can go there.'

'Actually –' I felt very awkward – 'umm, well, Issy's coming to stay.'

There was a long silence.

'I'm sorry. She was going to have to stay at the hotel otherwise and so I asked her,' I babbled.

'I see.' There was more than just a note of hostility in Ally's voice. 'So Harriet and I will have to wait another week before we see you.'

'Ally,' I said pleadingly, 'don't be like that. You know I want to see you and Harriet.' I had an idea. 'Maybe you could come here and meet Issy.'

'I guess,' Ally said slowly. I could tell she was thinking about. 'Or I suppose Issy could come and sleep over at Harriet's too. I know Harriet said Emily's away for the weekend, so there's an extra room. I'm sure Mr Chase won't mind.'

I blinked. Issy, Ally, Harriet and I all having a sleep-over together. I couldn't quite imagine it. But, then, why not? Issy was really nice. Ally and Harriet were sure to like her and I'd love for them all to be friends.

'OK,' I said, feeling suddenly excited. 'I'll ask Harriet.'

'Ring her now,' Ally urged.

I did and, as I'd expected, Harriet agreed immediately. 'It'll be really nice to meet Issy. She sounds fun.'

'She is,' I enthused. 'We'll have the best time.'

'When do you want to come over?'

I thought. 'Well, we should finish filming about two, which means we'll be at mine just after three. How about we come round then?'

'Great,' Harriet said. 'Ally and I get back from the stables at three, so that's just perfect.'

'All right,' I said, feeling pleased. 'See you then.'

Chapter Thirteen

'Go on inside,' Mum said to Issy and me on Saturday afternoon as she parked the car outside our house. 'I've just got to post a letter. Jessica's in, so the house should be open.'

Issy heaved her bag out of the car. She seemed to have brought enough clothes for a week!

'This village is so sweet!' she said, looking round.

I was a bit surprised. I'd never really thought of Ashton as sweet. It was quite a large village, with three pubs, several shops, two churches and a school. However, probably to Issy, who was used to London, it would seem very small.

I opened the gate. Baxter and Wilson came flying down to meet us.

'It's OK, they're friendly,' I said, seeing Issy back off in alarm.

Baxter and Wilson crowded round her.

'They're very slobbery,' she said, trying to push them away from her smart black jeans.

'Sorry,' I said quickly. 'Come on, dogs.'

I pulled Baxter and Wilson away. They looked at me

in surprise. Normally my friends love saying hello to them. I gave them a quick pat and followed Issy into the kitchen.

'Do you want a drink?' I asked her.

She nodded and I opened the fridge.

'Your fridge is really small, isn't it?' she commented.

I looked at the fridge. It seemed normal-sized to me.

'We've got one of those huge American fridges,' Issy went on. 'It's massive and it's got an ice-dispenser and everything. You should tell your mum and dad to get one. They're loads better.' She looked round the kitchen. 'You've got lots of stuff in here, haven't you?' She didn't sound entirely impressed.

I looked round our cosy cream-painted kitchen and saw it through her eyes – the dusty beams, the white walls covered with pictures Jess, Tom and I had drawn when we were little, the stickers on the fridge, the fireplace covered with silly little souvenirs we'd bought back from family holidays and the pots and pans piled up on the pine shelves because there was no room in the cupboards for them. I guess it did look like a lot of stuff, but I liked it.

'What's your kitchen like?' I asked.

'Modern, sleek, lots of stainless steel,' Issy replied. 'Mum hates clutter.'

Just then Jessica came into the kitchen.

'Jess, this is Issy,' I said.

'Hello,' Jessica said flatly. It was obvious she was in a bad mood.

She opened the fridge and frowned. 'Where's the last strawberry yoghurt?'

'I ate it,' I replied.

Jessica glared at me. 'Sophie! You know I only like strawberry yoghurts. You could have taken the banana one! That's so unfair!'

I stared at her in surprise. It wasn't like Jessica to get mad about something so silly. 'It's just a yoghurt.'

'Yeah – my strawberry yoghurt,' Jessica said. 'I can't believe you,' she went on, shaking her head. 'Little Miss Film Star, always having to have what you want! Well, the rest of us do count, you know!' She stormed out of the room.

There was a stunned silence.

Issy raised her eyebrows. 'I thought you said your sister was nice.'

'She is,' I said quickly.

'She didn't seem it then,' Issy replied.

'I know, but she is,' I insisted. I was reeling from Jessica's attack, but even so I didn't like to hear her being criticized by someone else. 'She's just upset about Dan.'

Issy didn't look convinced. 'Yeah, right.'

I felt a flicker of anger but forced it back. It was different for Issy. She was an only child. She didn't have sisters and she didn't understand what it was like.

'Come on,' I said, trying not to feel irritated. 'Let's go to my room.'

Setting off for Harriet's, I felt nervous. What would Issy think of Ally and Harriet? What would they think of her? I really wanted them all to get along.

Harriet and Ally were watching for us from the front window. As soon as we turned up the driveway, they came running out.

I introduced them and we all went through to the back garden. As we did so, I saw that Issy was looking at Harriet with a slight frown on her face.

My heart sank. I knew exactly why Issy was looking like that. Harriet was looking her least cool. She never bothers much about clothes anyway and today it was if she had thrown on the first things she found in her wardrobe – a pair of turquoise shorts and an old T-shirt that had the words I LOVE HORSES printed on the front.

In contrast, Issy was looking amazing in a cropped white T-shirt, black Jasper Conran jeans with slits up the sides and red flips-flops. I began to wish that Harriet had put on something a little bit nicer.

'Dad's put the sprinkler out,' Harriet said eagerly. 'Should I go and turn it on.'

'Yeah!' Ally said.

We often play in Harriet's sprinkler when it's a hot day.

Harriet ran to the wall of the house and turned the tap. Jets of water started shooting out of the sprinkler. Ally and I squealed and dodged as water squirted in our direction.

The next minute, Harriet, Ally and I were all shouting and laughing as we tried to avoid the sprinkler. It was brilliant fun, but as I dodged into the middle and then ran out of the sprinkler's range I suddenly realized that Issy was standing to one side.

'Come on!' I said, running over to her.

Issy shook her head. 'I don't want to.'

'Why not?' I demanded.

'I just washed my hair. I don't want it to get wet.'

I stared. Was she being serious?

'I haven't got my hair-dryer or straighteners,' she said, seeing my expression. 'I always have to dry it properly or it goes frizzy.'

'Come on, you two!' Ally shouted at us as she jumped into the middle and ran out again.

'Don't go, Sophie,' Issy said to me.

I hesitated. I really wanted to join in, but it seemed mean leaving Issy by herself. 'I don't feel like playing,' I called reluctantly.

Ally and Harriet stopped. They looked surprised.

'Why?' Harriet asked.

'I . . . I just don't,' I lied quickly.

I had a feeling they wouldn't be too impressed if they

knew the real reason Issy didn't want to play and I so wanted them to like her.

'What do you want to do, then?' Ally asked, sounding a bit put out.

I shrugged. 'Can we get a drink or something?'

Harriet nodded. 'OK.'

We followed her into the house.

'Is this your kitchen?' Issy said, looking round in surprise.

Harriet looked confused. 'Yes. Why?'

'Nothing,' Issy said. 'It's just, well, it's a bit small, isn't it?'

I saw Harriet's face stiffen.

'It might be small, but it's really nice,' Ally said quickly.

'Yeah. I love the colour your dad's painted it,' I added, looking at the lilac walls.

'Yeah, it is nice,' Issy said. 'But where do you eat? There's no table.'

'We eat in the lounge,' Harriet replied, her cheeks flushing red.

She hurried to a cupboard and fetched four cans of Coke and some Kit-Kats. It was easy to see she was embarrassed.

'Should we go back outside?' I said quickly.

'Yes, let's,' Harriet mumbled.

Going back into the garden, we started to eat our

Kit-Kats. Ally started to nibble all the chocolate off, spitting each piece out on to the silver foil.

Issy looked at her in astonishment. 'What are you doing?'

I grinned at her face. Harriet and I often teased Ally about the way she bites the chocolate off biscuits first. 'Take no notice. That's the way Ally always eats Kit-Kats. For some reason she says it makes them taste better.'

'It does!' Ally said, laughing. 'You should try it,' she told Issy.

'Er – no thanks,' Issy said, raising her eyebrows. She smiled briefly, but as she looked away I caught an expression of real disgust on her face.

I turned quickly to Ally. From the frown on her face, it was clear she had seen it too. I felt a flicker of hurt loyalty. OK, Harriet and I teased Ally about it, but biting chocolate off a biscuit wasn't a really gross habit. I mean, it wasn't like she was eating maggots or something.

'It's been good at the riding school this week,' Harriet said quickly. 'Do you ever go horse-riding, Issy?'

'No,' Issy said.

'Oh . . . right,' Harriet said.

For a moment no one spoke.

'I need the loo,' Issy said, standing up.

'It's just through the kitchen,' I told her.

As soon as she was out of earshot I looked at the

others. 'So? What do you think?' I waited anxiously for their answers.

'She's OK,' Ally said slowly. 'But, well, she's a bit . . . snobby, isn't she?'

'No,' I said defensively.

'Why wouldn't she play in the sprinkler?' Harriet asked.

I hesitated. 'She didn't want to get her hair wet,' I said reluctantly.

Ally and Harriet exchanged meaningful glances.

'She has to blow-dry it,' I tried to explain. 'Or it goes frizzy.'

'Don't you think that's a bit vain, Sophie?' Harriet said slowly.

As she spoke, Issy came out of the house. 'What are you talking about?' she asked.

'Nothing,' I said quickly.

Issy looked at Harriet. I wondered whether she had overheard.

Just then, Mr Chase came into the garden. 'Hi, girls,' he said.

He was wearing old jeans and a frayed T-shirt that had the name of some ancient band on it. It was how he always dressed at weekends, but suddenly I found myself seeing him through Issy's eyes. What would she think of him?

'I'm just going to make some sandwiches,' he said. 'What would you like? Cheese, ham or salad?'

We all told him what we wanted – cheese salad for Issy, ham salad for me and Harriet, and plain ham for Ally.

'Right, I'll go and get something sorted out,' Mr Chase said. As he went to go, he smiled at me. 'Sorry to hear you can't come to Alton Towers next week, Sophie. Harriet says you'll be filming. Never mind, next time, eh?' And with that he walked back to the house.

Alton Towers? What was he talking about? I glanced at Ally and Harriet. They were looking mortified.

'Alton Towers!' I said, my skin feeling suddenly hot and prickly as I processed what Mr Chase had just said. 'Are you two going to Alton Towers?'

Harriet blushed. 'Yes. We were going to tell you, Soph – we only just decided yesterday.'

'We knew you wouldn't be able to come, that's why we didn't ring you,' Ally said.

My stomach felt like it had just dropped down a lift shaft. I couldn't believe it. Ally, Harriet and I had been talking about going to Alton Towers together for ages. We'd even planned the rides we would go on. Now they were going without me! Hurt overwhelmed me.

Harriet saw my face. 'I think I'll just go and help Dad with the sandwiches,' she stammered, looking very embarrassed.

'I'll help too,' Ally said hastily, also jumping to her feet.

I stared after them. I couldn't believe it. How could they?

Issy leaned forward. 'God, did you see what Harriet's dad was wearing?' she said in an undertone. 'I mean, how sad? Does he really think it's cool to go around wearing a T-shirt with the name of a band that no one's heard of?'

I didn't reply. I was still reeling with hurt and shock.

'Imagine having your dad dressed like that,' Issy went on. 'It must be *so* embarrassing. It's no wonder Harriet's a fashion disaster herself — turquoise shorts . . . I mean, pur-lease!'

Despite myself I giggled. Part of me felt mean laughing, but right at the moment I was so upset by Harriet and Ally's behaviour that I didn't care.

'Surely she can see how awful she looks,' Issy went on. 'She and her dad. I mean, don't they have any mirrors?' She snickered. 'Probably not. The house is really skanky too.'

I stopped laughing. Issy had gone too far. But before I could say anything in Harriet's defence, someone else spoke.

'You cow, Sophie!'

I swung round. Ally was holding a tray of drinks and crisps, a look of outrage on her face.

Chapter Fourteen

Ally dumped the tray on the grass. 'How *dare* you laugh at Harriet and her dad and her house!' she exclaimed.

'I wasn't,' I protested. 'Ally –'

'I don't want to hear it,' Ally interrupted. 'You're both horrible! You *and* your stuck-up friend!' She pointed to Issy.

Issy got to her feet. 'Me?'

'Yes, you!' Ally retorted. 'You might be famous, but you're a snobby, stuck-up –'

'Ally!' I exclaimed.

'Just leave her,' Issy said grabbing my arm. 'Come on. Let's go back to yours, Soph.'

'Let's go back to yours, Soph,' Ally mimicked Issy's voice. 'Yeah, go on, Sophie. You go off with *her*.' Anger blazed in her eyes. 'It's obvious Harriet and I aren't good enough for you any more! You never ring us or come and see us. We're just not famous enough, are we?'

Just then Harriet came out of the house. 'What's happening?' she demanded in astonishment.

I looked from her to Ally. I was desperate to explain that it had all just been a mistake, to say that, yes, I had been horrible, but it was only because I was feeling hurt. But that would mean admitting to Harriet what Issy and I had been saying.

'Come on!' Issy insisted, pulling my arm. She glared at Ally. 'I'm not going to stay here and be insulted.'

'Good,' Ally said. 'Cos we don't want you to stay. Go off and have little snobby mean talks.' She linked arms with Harriet. 'We don't want you here – either of you.'

'Well, that's just fine by us!' I said, feeling angry myself as I saw what a united twosome they made. 'Come on, Issy!'

We marched up the garden and out of the gate.

'Who does she think she is?' Issy raged as we left. 'Talking to me like that? I can't *believe* she's your friend.'

'Ex-friend,' I said angrily.

But as we started to walk back to mine, my temper cooled and I began to feel distinctly shaky. How could I have laughed about Harriet like that? I felt awful – mean and disloyal. My cheeks flushed as I saw Ally's face in my mind as she overheard. The feeling was almost too much to bear. I was horrible – *horrible*! I wanted to run back straight away and apologize, but my feet just kept walking along the street. I couldn't go back. Not now.

'You don't need friends like that,' Issy told me. 'They're just jealous because they've got such sad boring lives. You should forget about them.'

I nodded. I wanted to believe it. But I couldn't. It was Ally and Harriet we were talking about.

Issy smiled. 'It'll be much more fun just the two of us today. You'll see.'

Mum was really surprised when we got home so early. 'What's happened?' she said. 'I thought you were sleeping over at the Chases' house.' She looked at my face. 'Have you had an argument with Ally and Harriet?'

'No,' I lied, not wanting to have to talk about it. 'Issy and I just thought we'd rather stay here.'

Mum looked at me closely, but then, to my relief, she dropped the subject. 'So, what are you planning to do for the rest of the afternoon?' she asked.

I shrugged.

'Well, how about giving me a hand?' Mum suggested. 'I've got three Persian cats who need grooming and four guinea pigs to clean out. Fancy coming to help me?'

'OK,' Issy and I agreed.

We spent the rest of the afternoon helping Mum. I had a feeling that Issy was quite bored. She groomed the cats but only for a few minutes and then she spent the rest of the time sunbathing while I cleaned out the guinea pigs. Afterwards we dropped some of Mum's leaflets in at people's houses and then we set up my bedroom for our sleepover.

It felt very strange having a sleepover without Ally or Harriet. Issy wanted to read Jessica's magazines and put make-up on. She had brought some CDs with her so we played them and made up some dance routines. It was fun, but I did miss slobbing around and stuffing my face the way I usually did with the others.

Still, Issy seemed to enjoy herself. 'We've got to do this again,' she said as we finally went to bed. 'It's been fun.'

I nodded, but I couldn't stop thinking about Ally and Harriet. It had never been the two of them against me. It was a horrible lonely feeling. Maybe if I rang them in the morning and apologized, we could make up and forget about it.

But what about Alton Towers? A lump swelled in my throat. It was no use. Even if I apologized, it didn't change the fact that our friendship had changed. It wasn't the three of us any more. It was them and me.

Turning my face into the pillow, hot tears prickled down my cheeks.

'Thanks for having me, Mrs Tennison,' Issy said politely as she got out of the car at Stanton Hall the next day. 'I had a great time.' She grinned at me. 'See you tomorrow, Soph.'

'Yeah, bye,' I said, trying to smile.

Issy seemed to think that I should just forget about Ally and Harriet. But it wasn't that easy. They were my best friends. *Or they used to be*, I thought unhappily as I got back into the car.

'Got any plans for today?' Mum asked, looking across at me as she started the engine.

I shook my head.

'You're not going to see Ally and Harriet?' Mum said.

She spoke casually, but I knew she was trying to find out what was going on.

'No,' I said.

Mum glanced at me. 'Have you fallen out with them?'

There was no point in denying it for a second time. After all, she was going to find out sooner or later. I nodded.

'It'll blow over,' Mum said.

I swallowed. 'It won't.'

To my relief, Mum didn't just laugh it off. 'Why? What's happened?' She looked at me shrewdly. 'Didn't they like Issy?'

'No – but then it wasn't just that,' I added quickly. 'There was other stuff.'

'What stuff?'

I wanted to tell Mum everything. But I couldn't. How could I admit that I'd been so mean about Harriet? 'I . . . I don't want to talk about it,' I muttered.

Mum didn't say anything for a moment. But then, to my relief, she nodded. 'OK, but if you do want to talk you know I'm here. And, Sophie . . .'

'Yes.'

'Don't throw your friendship away over a silly argument. Friends are very important, particularly good friends like Ally and Harriet.'

I nodded and we drove on in silence.

I hung around the house for the rest of the morning, feeling very bored. Several times I went to the phone but then stopped as I realized I had no one to ring. Issy was filming and I couldn't exactly ring Ally or Harriet. I wondered what Ally had told Harriet about the fight. I hoped she hadn't told her about me laughing at her. I didn't think I could bear that.

After lunch, I took Baxter and Wilson for a walk. However, to my horror, just as I was going past the newsagent's, Ally and Harriet came out.

Harriet was in front. She stopped so abruptly when she saw me that Ally walked into the back of her.

'What . . .' Ally started to exclaim and then she saw me.

I looked at Harriet; her hazel eyes were confused and hurt.

I swallowed. *I'm sorry!* The words were there, on the tip of my tongue . . .

'Excuse me, dears.' Mrs Wilson, a lady who lived in our street, was trying to leave the newsagent's, but Ally and Harriet were blocking the doorway. 'Can I squeeze past?'

Ally grabbed Harriet's arm. 'We're just going.' She

shot a horrible look at me. 'There's a nasty smell around here.' They both put their noses in the air and marched past me without a word.

My eyes blurred with tears and, pulling hard on the dogs' leads, I ran all the way home.

It was a huge relief to get back on to the film set on Monday and to be able to think about something else. I threw myself into acting and tried not to think about Ally and Harriet.

In the morning we were filming a scene in a corridor and the corridor that was being used was hot from the lights.

As I waited between takes, Jules came over. 'Just a bit of powder to take off any shine on your face,' she said as she expertly whisked a towel over my costume and brushed some powder on to my face.

'Here's a chair,' Margaret said, coming over. 'Sit down and rest for a moment.'

As I sat down, Cathy brought me a carton of Ribena. 'Here, I thought you could use this, Sophie.'

'Thanks.' I smiled gratefully.

Laurence walked past. 'That last take was great, Sophie. You had just the right expression in your voice. We should have this scene wrapped up in no time. Well done.'

As he strode off I felt my problems at home fade. On the set, people fussed over me and thought I was important. So what if I'd argued with Ally and Harriet? I didn't need them.

Really? a little voice in my head said.

Really, I thought.

Chapter Fifteen

The next three weeks flew by until, almost before I knew it, it was the last day filming at Stanton Hall. I still had some more to do – five days on location in Lincolnshire and then a week at the film studio near Birmingham. But it wasn't going to be the same. I'd got used to being at Stanton Hall each day and I was really going to miss it.

None of the extras was needed for any more filming and so Joan and Margaret organized a goodbye party in the green room. There were sandwiches, crisps and cakes, and all the adults who weren't needed on set joined in too. Even Georgina came. She and Issy had never really made friends with any of the extras, but after I had insisted on going to the rounders game they had started being a bit more willing to join in on the days the other girls were on the set. I found their attitude really strange. I enjoyed doing things with the others. I didn't understand why they didn't.

'I'm going to really miss coming here,' Justine said to me as we helped ourselves to food. 'It's weird to think that in just a few weeks we'll be starting at Charles Hope, isn't it?'

Weird? It was more than just weird. I couldn't even *begin* to imagine it! It was like something that would happen to some other Sophie Tennison, not to me. I pushed the thought to the back of my mind. It was way too scary to think about.

At 6 o'clock the party broke up and everyone was collected by their parents. There was lots of hugging and exchanging addresses and phone numbers.

'Well, I guess I'll see you in a few weeks, Sophie,' Justine said when her mum arrived.

'Yeah, see you.'

We looked at each other awkwardly. I wanted to step forward and hug her just like I'd been hugging everyone else, but there was a bit of me that found the whole idea just too strange. OK, being on the set wasn't like real life and we'd become almost like friends in the last couple of weeks, but hug *Justine*?

Justine seemed to find the idea of us hugging equally freaky. She hastily stepped back as I hesitated.

'Well . . . er . . . I'll see you, then,' she said, swinging her bag on to her shoulder. 'Bye, Sophie.'

'Bye.' I nodded. 'Have a good holiday.'

She hurried over to her mum's car. I waved, wondering what things would be like when we started at school. Would we be friends or would we go back to being enemies? I wasn't sure, but I did know I didn't want to think about filming ending and real life starting again. Forgetting Justine and school for the moment, I went to find Issy.

'I can't believe I'm not going to be seeing you for a whole week,' I said.

Issy wasn't going to be needed until we started at the film studio.

'I know,' Issy said. 'I'll really miss you, Soph. You're my best friend.'

I felt a warm glow. 'You're mine too.'

'And you promise you'll ring me every day?' Issy demanded.

I smiled at her. 'I will.'

I didn't do much at the weekend. I didn't want to go out in case I met Ally and Harriet. It didn't matter how often I told myself that I didn't care about them, I did care. I was missing them really badly and I didn't want to see them out in the village together. So I stayed in learning my lines. It was really boring, but then on Sunday, just as I was about to leave for Lincolnshire, something good actually happened. I was opening the car door when Jessica came hurrying down the road. Her eyes were shining, her cheeks flushed.

'Soph!' she exclaimed, breaking into a run. 'Guess what?'

'What?' I demanded.

'I've just seen Dan and I think we've made up!'

'Really?' I gasped. ' What happened?'

'I was just coming back from Nicole's when I saw him posting a letter. I went over and he actually talked to me instead of just walking off. I told him how I wished the whole Zak thing had never happened and he said he's been missing me. He's asked me out tonight!' She hugged me. 'I'm so excited.'

'That's brilliant!' I told her, hugging her in return. 'I knew you'd get back together!'

'Into the car, Soph!' Dad said, coming out of the house with my suitcase.

'See you in a few days,' I said to Jessica.

'Yeah,' she replied. 'Have a good time filming.'

'I will,' I said, grinning.

But being away on location wasn't nearly as much fun as I'd thought it was going to be. Margaret made me go to bed at 9 o'clock every night because I had to be up at 6 every morning. Even worse, whenever I tried to ring Issy she always seemed to be out, and the only time she rang me back I was filming.

By the time my five days of filming were over I was longing to get home. On the final day, it took us four hours to shoot a short scene. Everything seemed to go wrong. It rained, an aeroplane flew overhead and then some workmen started drilling in a street nearby. As we repeated our lines over and over again and stood around waiting for the light to be right for filming, everyone grew more and more short-tempered and I found myself wishing that we were back at Stanton Hall.

During the breaks I sat with Gillian in the green room – a mobile home type of caravan.

'This is when I remember why I don't like filming,' she said, drinking a cup of black coffee with a sigh.

'Mum told me you mainly act in the theatre,' I said, sipping my can of Coke.

She nodded. 'I've done a few films but I prefer acting on the stage.'

'Why?' I said.

She smiled. 'There's just something about being in front of a live audience. Feeling the play change every night. There's nothing like it.'

'But don't you mind about not being famous?' I asked curiously.

Gillian looked genuinely surprised. 'No. In fact, that's one of the reasons I prefer theatre. In the theatre you're judged more on your talent and less on your celebrity status.' She shook her head. 'I've never wanted fame.'

I frowned. Surely everyone wanted to be famous?

Gillian saw my confusion. 'Fame comes at a price, Sophie,' she said, her eyes holding mine. 'And that price is your privacy. It might not seem important to you now, but as soon as you become a so-called famous person people feel they have a right to you and your family and your life. But I've always tried to keep my personal life – my family and friends – separate from my professional life – my acting.'

'Why?'

'My family and my friends are my rock,' she said. 'They don't care how successful I am, they are always there for me no matter what I do.' She frowned and took a sip of her coffee. 'Acting friendships are fickle. It's the nature of the job. Every time you start a new production you have to make a new set of friends. At first, of course, you try and keep up all the friend-ships you've made, but you soon realize that you just can't do it and you develop the talent for getting on with people while you work with them but not becoming too deeply attached.' She looked at me. 'I'm not say-ing all acting friendships are shallow – I've made a few very good friends over the years – but it's just that, if you're wise, you'll realize that most acting friendships don't last any longer than the production you're doing. Unless of course you meet up with the same person again.'

I considered what she was saying. I supposed she was right. I couldn't see me staying in touch with Georgina at all, or even the friends I'd made among the extras apart from Justine. But she wasn't right about Issy. Even though we hadn't spoken to each other all week, I knew our friendship was *definitely* going to be one of those that lasted.

Just then Cathy came into the caravan. 'The light's OK again.'

Gillian smiled at me. 'Back to work,' she said.

'That's a wrap!' Gary called through the megaphone later that afternoon.

There was a spontaneous cheer from all the crew. Our last scene in Lincolnshire had just been filmed. I joined in with the cheer. I was very glad the week was over. It hadn't been much fun at all.

Laurence stretched. 'Thanks very much, guys. I'll see you on Monday at the studio.'

I headed back to my trailer – the large caravan that was my dressing room on set. To my delight, Dad was waiting for me. He pulled me into a bear hug.

'Sophie! How are you?' he said.

I snuggled into his arms in relief. 'Ready to go home.'

✦

Chapter Sixteen

As I walked through the gate, Baxter and Wilson hurtled down to greet me. A sandy-coloured dog who looked like a small, fat Border collie came trotting down the yard after them.

'Hello, there,' I said, stroking her along with Baxter and Wilson. 'Who are you?'

'This is Sally, one of your mum's charges,' Dad said, scratching her silky ears. 'She's staying for another ten days. She's a bit of a handful though. She's been chewing things up and weeing on the floor. Her owner, Mrs Ling, only got her from a rescue kennel a month or so ago and your mum thinks being in another new house so soon has upset her.'

'Oh, Sally,' I said, scratching her ears.

Sally licked my hand and wagged her plumy tail.

'Sophie, you're home,' Mum said, coming out to greet me. She hugged me. 'How are you?'

'Fine,' I said.

'I see you've met Sally.'

'She's very fat,' I said, looking at the plump little dog.

'I know,' Mum said. 'But very sweet.'

Just then the phone rang. Dad answered it.

'Sophie, it's for you!' he called. 'It's Issy.'

At last! I ran to the phone.

'Issy! Where have you been?' I demanded. 'I've been trying to ring you all week.'

'I know. I'm sorry, Soph. I got your messages but I've been so busy. Forgive me?'

'Of course,' I said, just happy to hear her voice. 'So how are you?'

'Brilliant!' Issy sounded really bubbly. 'You'll never guess what!'

'What?' I demanded

'I've got a screen test tomorrow for a role in a new TV series. It's a drama about these four children who travel back in time. The director's seen me in some of the other stuff I've done and he's really keen to use me. Isn't it great?'

A screen test! I felt a flood of conflicting emotions — delight but also intense, stabbing jealousy.

'Sophie?' Issy said.

I realized that she was waiting for me to say something. 'It's brilliant,' I told her, trying to feel pleased. 'I hope you get it.'

'How was Issy?' Mum asked when I put the phone down.

'She's got a screen test tomorrow. It's not fair, Mum,' I said in despair. 'My life's going to be so boring after the film finishes.'

Mum smiled. 'Starting at secondary school will hardly be boring.'

Secondary school! Help! Images flashed in front of my mind – teachers shouting, getting lost, being late, not knowing anyone. I felt like curling up in panic. It had been scary enough thinking about going to Charles Hope when Ally and Harriet had been my friends. The thought of going with no friends made me feel positively sick.

'It's only ten days now until you start,' Mum said, going to the sink. 'We'll have to do something about getting your uniform.'

I didn't want to think about it. I jumped up. 'I'm going to go and unpack.'

I sorted my clothes out and was helping Mum peel some potatoes for supper when Dan came round.

'Hi, Mrs Tennison. Hi, Soph.'

It was really nice to see him again. I grinned at him. 'Hello.'

I'd spoken to Jessica on the phone while I'd been away so I knew they'd officially started going out together again.

Just then Jessica came into the room. She said hello to him but hung back. There was a moment's awkward pause. I frowned. Now that they had got back together, I'd expected them to be all lovey-dovey and soppy, but they weren't at all. In fact, they both seemed tense around each other.

'Should we go and watch TV in the playroom?' Jessica said.

Dan nodded and they went through into the small room off the kitchen that used to be our playroom when we were little but now has a TV in it and usually a load of laundry.

Leaving the casserole to cook, Mum went through to the lounge. I hung around in the kitchen wondering about Jess and Dan. Feeling curious, I went to the playroom door and peeped in. Whenever they had watched TV together before they had usually spent most of the time laughing and making sarcastic remarks about the programmes. Now they were sitting about a foot apart, not saying anything. What was up with them?

Jessica glanced at Dan. 'Would you like a biscuit?'

'Yes, please,' he said, his voice weirdly formal.

I jumped away from the door as Jessica came through and made a big show of getting something from the fridge so she wouldn't think I'd been spying on her.

She got the biscuits out of the cupboard, but as she turned to go back I couldn't stop myself from saying something. 'What's going on?'

She stopped. 'What do you mean?'

'With you and Dan,' I whispered. 'You're acting really strange.'

For a moment I thought she was going to tell me to mind my own business but then she sighed. 'I don't know,' she confided in a low voice. 'I thought everything would be just the same when we started going out again, but it's different. It's like something's changed. He won't talk to me like he used to. I feel like . . . like there's this barrier there.' She ran a hand through her hair. 'I don't know what to do. I want it to be just like it was.'

'It will be,' I said.

'I hope so.' Jessica sighed, then she turned and went into the playroom.

Chapter Seventeen

'So how was the screen test?' I asked Issy on Monday morning.

I'd thought about it and I'd made up my mind to be a good friend and be totally supportive of her.

'Brilliant!' Issy enthused. 'Now I've just got to wait for the phone call.'

She was wearing a brown suede miniskirt – new – and a black cut-off top – also new.

'It would be such an amazing role to get,' she went on. 'It's a pity you didn't audition – Georgina was there.'

I stared. 'Georgina was having a screen test?'

Issy nodded. 'For a different role from me.'

Jealousy overwhelmed me and my good intentions went out of the window. Georgina had been at the screen test too! How unfair was that?

Issy checked her reflection in the mirror. 'I wish Margaret would hurry up. I want to go and explore.'

There was a knock on the door.

'Ready to go to Make-up?' Margaret asked, coming in.

'Definitely,' Issy said, jumping up.

We'd been given strict instructions that we weren't allowed to go out of the dressing room on our own. The film-studio complex the remaining scenes were going to be filmed at was set in 300 acres of grounds and there were other TV and film companies working there, not just us, so we had to be chaperoned wherever we went.

We followed Margaret eagerly down the corridor past the other dressing rooms, past the Wardrobe department and on to the set. I stared. It was a huge space, with loads of people hurrying around. It had an enormously high ceiling, concrete floor and white walls. In the centre of the room cameras and lights surrounded a set. I didn't have to ask which set it was supposed to be.

'Sara's attic room,' I breathed, walking forward.

It looked exactly like a proper room: it had floorboards and peeling plaster on the walls, a window and an old iron bed. The only difference between it and a normal room was that it had just three walls and it didn't have a ceiling.

'It looks really good,' I said.

Margaret smiled. 'Come on. Make-up's this way.'

'Not many more days to go now,' Jules said as she applied a final smudge of blusher to my cheeks. 'How long till you finish filming?'

'Just a week,' I replied.

'So, is it back to school, then?' Sandy asked, spraying hairspray over Issy.

'Hopefully not for me,' Issy replied. 'Or at least not for long if I get this part in the TV series.'

'How about you, Sophie?' Jules asked. 'What are you doing after this?'

I wished I could say that I was going to be in some TV series or other. 'Nothing,' I admitted.

'I'm sure something will turn up,' Jules said. She brushed my face with a large brush. 'There, you're all done.'

As I stood up, the door opened and Georgina came in.

Jules smiled. 'Come and sit down, Georgina. I've just finished Sophie.'

Georgina came over. 'Any news on the screen test yet?' she said to Issy as she sat down.

Issy shook her head.

'It'll be cool if we both get parts, won't it?' Georgina said.

I expected Issy to just shrug, but to my surprise she didn't. 'Yeah, it'll be great,' she enthused.

I looked at her in surprise. She sounded like she meant it.

'All done,' Sandy said to Issy.

The door opened and Margaret looked in. 'Sophie, you'd better come and get changed now.'

I got up. 'Are you coming?' I asked Issy.

She hesitated. 'I think I'll stay here.' She looked at Margaret. 'I don't need to get changed yet, do I?'

'No,' Margaret replied. 'You're not needed for a bit. You can stay if you want.'

'OK, I'll stay here, then.' Issy sat down again and turned to Georgina. 'So what was your screen test like?'

'Good,' Georgina said.

'Mine too,' Issy said. 'Which scene did you do?'

'Sophie, come on,' Margaret said.

I was kept really busy all day. Sometimes when I was filming Issy came on set to watch me, but at other times she hung round with Georgina. Watching them giggling together at the side of the set in the afternoon, I felt like the odd one out.

'You're quiet,' Cathy said to me on the way home.

I shrugged.

'Are you tired?' she asked sympathetically. 'It's been a long day, hasn't it?'

I nodded and Cathy didn't say anything more until we got home.

'Get an early night,' she said. 'I'll see you tomorrow at eight.'

'Thanks for the lift,' I said as I got out.

Sally trotted over to me when I opened the gate, but there was no sign of Baxter and Wilson. I guessed Mum or Dad had taken them out for a walk. I walked up the yard and pushed open the kitchen door. As I did so I heard the sound of two raised voices.

'I was not flirting!'

'No? It sure looked like flirting to me!'

I stopped in the doorway. Jessica and Dan were standing either side of the kitchen table glaring at each other. They were so busy arguing they barely noticed me.

'I was just being friendly,' Jessica said. 'He was Raj's cousin. He didn't know anyone.'

'So you went out of your way to get to know him,' Dan said, his eyes angry.

'Dan!' Jessica said in frustration. 'What's got into you? I was just being nice.' She stared at him. 'This is about Zak, isn't it? You think I'm going to go off with someone else.'

'Well, it wouldn't be the first time, would it?' Dan said.

I thought Jessica was going to explode, but she didn't. She took a deep breath and stepped towards him. 'Dan,' she said, her voice quieter, 'if you don't trust me we can't go out together. You've *got* to start trusting me again.'

Dan met her gaze. 'Easier said than done,' he said, and, turning, he walked past me without even saying hello or goodbye.

As the gate banged shut Jessica sank down on a chair and put her head in her hands.

'What was all that about?' I asked.

'I don't want to talk about it,' Jessica said, and, pushing back her chair, she strode out of the room.

I stared after her and then went to get a drink. As I shut the fridge, I heard the gate opening. Looking out of the window I saw Mum coming into the yard with Baxter and Wilson.

'Hi,' I called, opening the back door.

'Hello, love,' Mum said as the dogs charged up to me, their tails wagging, their tongues hanging out. 'How are you?'

'OK,' I said, scratching Wilson's and Baxter's ears.

'Back, dogs,' she said, pushing past them to get into the house.

I noticed she looked harassed. 'What's the matter?' I asked.

'Oh, it's just been one of those days,' Mum said, shaking her head. 'Sally tore up a pile of newspapers in the lounge and then she chewed up one of Jessica's trainers.'

'Oh, no,' I said.

'Yes,' Mum said. 'Jessica wasn't best pleased. Anyway, how was filming?'

'OK,' I said. 'Busy.'

'Do you want me to help you go through your lines tonight?' Mum said.

'Yes, please,' I said.

The kitchen door opened and Tom appeared.

'Hi, Soph,' he said. 'Mum, can you take me round to Nick's tonight?'

'Again?' Mum said. 'But you were there all morning.'

'I know,' Tom said, 'but this guy from a new club in town is coming to listen to us next weekend, so we want to get as much practice in as possible. If he likes us we could get to play at some under-eighteen evenings.'

'Oh, Tom, I really don't want to go out again tonight,' Mum said. 'I've been running around all day and I've promised Sophie I'll help her with her lines.'

'But I've got to go,' Tom said. He frowned. 'I bet if I was Sophie you would take me. You're always running round after her!'

'Tom, that's not true . . .' Mum began.

Just then Jessica came into the kitchen. It was obvious that she was in a bad mood.

'Mum, is it OK if Nicole and Laura sleep over tonight?'

Mum shook her head. 'Not tonight, Jess. I'm shattered.'

'We're not going to disturb you,' Jessica said. 'We'll be in my bedroom.'

'I know, but I'd just rather they didn't come round. Sophie's got her lines to learn and she's got an early start tomorrow.'

Jessica glared at me. 'Oh, and of course we can't do anything to upset precious little Sophie.'

'Jessica!' Mum said, looking cross. 'Be reasonable! Sophie's working hard – she needs to have a quiet evening. Nicole and Laura can stay another time.'

'But I've already said they can come round tonight,' Jessica said. 'What am I going to tell them?'

'That I've said no,' Mum said sharply. 'And you shouldn't have arranged it without asking first.'

'But I need to see them,' Jessica said. 'You don't understand.'

'The answer's no, Jessica,' Mum said.

'This is so unfair!' Jessica exploded. 'I bet if I were Sophie you'd say yes. Sophie gets whatever she wants.'

'Too true,' Tom muttered, and they marched from the room.

Mum stared after her. 'Honestly! Teenagers!'

I sat down at the table, feeling hurt. Tom and Jessica had been really unkind. They didn't usually gang up on me.

Mum saw my face. 'Oh, love, don't get upset. They didn't mean what they said. They're just cross because they can't have what they want.'

'They're both really mad at me,' I said.

'No, they're not,' Mum said. 'They're just taking their bad moods out on you.' She sighed. 'Remember, it's not easy for them watching you doing this film and being the centre of attention.'

'But I thought they were pleased I was doing the film,' I said.

'They are,' Mum replied. 'But that doesn't mean they don't feel a little bit jealous. You're their younger sister. Try and see things from their point of view.'

'They hate me,' I said miserably.

Mum smiled. 'Don't be silly. They might be a bit grumpy at the moment, but deep down they love you and they'll always be there for you.'

I swallowed. I knew she was right, but it didn't change the fact that right now Jessica and Tom were both in moods with me.

'Don't worry about it,' Mum said. 'Take your things upstairs and then we'll go through your lines before dinner.'

I went upstairs. Jessica and Tom's bedroom doors were shut tight and music was blaring out. Despite Mum's words, I went into my room and sat down on my bed feeling thoroughly miserable. Ally and Harriet weren't my friends any more, Jessica and Tom weren't speaking to me, filming was about to end and I was going to have to start secondary school. Could life get any worse?

Dimly I heard the phone ringing. It stopped and then Mum called up the stairs, 'Sophie, it's Issy on the phone for you.'

I went to get the phone in Mum and Dad's bedroom.

'Sophie, hi!' Issy said. She sounded really excited. 'I just *had* to ring you. I've got the part in the TV series and, guess what, Georgina's going to be in it too!'

For a moment my head seemed to swim. Issy had got the part! She was going to be in a TV show while I had to go back to school.

'Isn't it brilliant?' Issy bubbled.

I could tell she was waiting for me to say something. 'Yeah, it's great.' I forced the words out of me. 'Well done, Is.'

Issy started going on about how much fun it would be and how glad she was that she wasn't going to just go back to school. Luckily she didn't seem to expect me to say much. As her voice flooded into my ear I tried very hard to be happy for her, but it was really difficult.

After five minutes I couldn't bear it any more. 'I'd better go,' I lied. 'Mum needs me to help get supper ready.'

'OK,' Issy said. 'I've got to go round to Georgie's room. We're going to celebrate. See you tomorrow!'

'Yeah,' I said, 'see you.'

I put the phone down. Icy fingers seemed to curl round my heart. *Georgie's* room! Since when had Georgina been Georgie?

Life, I realized, had just got *much* worse.

Chapter Eighteen

Over the next two days things didn't improve. Jessica and Tom virtually ignored me and Issy seemed to be getting friendlier with Georgina all the time. She even arranged for Georgina to come and share our dressing room.

'She's not that bad,' she said to me. 'And we're going to have to be friends when we do *Back in Time* together, so I may as well start being friendly now.'

Fine, but did she have to be quite *that* friendly?

On Friday I finally managed to get Issy on her own for once. Georgina was only needed for a short time in the morning and then she was taken back to the hotel. Issy and I had lunch together and, as we gossiped about the fact that Jules and Gary had officially started going out, I felt happier than I had done in days. Issy obviously did still want to be my best friend after all. But I couldn't stop thinking about what Gillian had said when we were away on location.

'Issy,' I said as we walked back to the green room, 'when I was in Lincolnshire I was talking to Gillian and she said that people often don't stay friends when a film ends. Don't you think that's an odd thing to say?'

I looked at Issy hopefully. I was sure she was going to say it was rubbish, but my heart sank as she nodded.

'I guess that is true,' she said. 'I mean, it's not like you stop being friends, but it's just that you're not best friends any more. You make new best friends with the people you work with next.'

I stared at her. 'But what about us?' I wanted to say. However, she looked so calm and unbothered that I just couldn't. 'Do . . . do you think we'll stay friends?' I said.

She grinned. 'Of course – we're best friends.'

I wanted to believe her, but part of me had a horrid feeling that it wasn't true.

'Here we are,' Cathy said as she pulled up outside my house that evening.

I woke with a start, my head hurting from where I had been resting it against the car window. I tried to focus my sleep-scrambled thoughts.

'Thanks for the lift,' I mumbled, wondering how long I'd been asleep.

'See you tomorrow,' Cathy said as I got out of the car.

I waved her off and then turned to go in through the gate, but then I stopped. Ally and Harriet were coming up the road together with Ally's dog. I hadn't seen them for ages and suddenly I felt an overwhelming desire to talk to them. I went over.

'Hi,' I said impulsively.

They stopped dead. A look of relief leapt into Harriet's eyes and a smile started on Ally's lips and for a moment I thought everything was going to be all right. But then Ally's smile turned into a scowl.

I tried to fill the awkward silence. 'What have you been doing?'

Ally ignored me. 'Come on, Harriet,' she said, tugging at Harriet's arm. 'Let's go.' She shot me a withering look.

Harriet seemed to hesitate for a moment but then, tossing back her ponytail, she nodded and they marched on without saying another word.

I felt like I had been kicked in the stomach. Tears sprang to my eyes as I watched them walk away without a backward glance. It was hopeless. We were *never* going to be friends again.

Dashing away my tears with the back of my hand, I went through the gate. My life was horrible. I hated it. The dogs crowded round me, but I felt too miserable to even say hello to them.

I opened the kitchen door. Mum was standing by the table mopping up a puddle on the floor and Jessica was picking up a pile of clothes that for some reason seemed to be scattered over the floor.

'Sophie, don't let the dogs in!' Mum cried quickly.

But it was too late. In his excitement, Baxter bounced straight into the bucket she was using.

'No!' Mum exclaimed as the bucket went flying and water spilt all over the floor, splashing Jessica and the clothes on the way.

'Sophie, you idiot!' Jessica exclaimed.

'Sorry!' I gasped.

'For goodness' sake, Sophie!' Mum shouted. 'Get the dogs out!'

Mum almost never shouted. Seeing how stressed she looked, I grabbed the dogs and hauled them outside by their collars, shutting the door on their eager faces.

'This is the last straw,' Mum exclaimed, looking round at the chaos.

'What . . . what's going on?' I stammered.

Mum took a deep breath. 'It has *not* been a good day.' Running a hand over her face, she took another breath as if to calm herself and then started mopping up the water on the floor. 'First of all, Jessica and I went round to see the three cats I'm looking after only to find that one of them had escaped. We spent two hours searching for it. Eventually we found it under the shed, but it took us another hour to coax it out.'

'Then we came back and found that Sally had done another puddle on the floor,' Jessica said. 'And she's pulled all the clean laundry out of the playroom and tried to make a bed.'

'This place is a tip,' Mum said. 'Could you put the laundry on again, Jessica, and Sophie, would you mind taking Sally out for a walk?'

I started to nod, but then I remembered that Ally and Harriet were out walking Ally's dog. I didn't want to risk bumping into them. 'Do I have to?' I said. 'Can –'

Before I could say, 'Can I do the washing or mop the floor instead?' Jessica snapped, 'Yes, you do have to! Can't you stop being selfish for even one moment?'

'That's enough, Jess,' Mum said quickly. She looked at me. 'It would be a really big help, Sophie. I know you must be tired, but –'

'That's not why . . .' I broke off. Now wasn't the time to go into my encounter with Ally and Harriet. 'Yeah, I'll take them,' I said, reaching for the leads from the door.

I went outside. Baxter and Wilson came charging over to me, but Sally stayed sitting where she was.

'Come on,' I said, putting her lead on. 'Walkies.'

She got up reluctantly. She walked a few paces and then stopped.

'Come on,' I said, tugging at the lead.

She whined and sat down. I went inside again.

'I don't think Sally wants to go for a walk.'

'Just take her, please,' Mum said.

I shrugged and went back out to the dogs.

Leading them out of the gate, I turned the opposite direction from the way Ally and Harriet had gone.

'Come on,' I said, clicking my tongue to Sally.

She followed me reluctantly. We walked round the church, but after we'd been going five minutes I noticed that Sally was starting to pant. I stopped and she immediately sat down and whined. I watched her, looking at her sides moving in and out and her pink tongue hanging out of her mouth. Maybe she was ill. I hesitated and then headed back home.

'Sophie!' Jessica exclaimed as I opened the door.

'It's Sally,' I said quickly. 'I don't think she's very well. She keeps whining and sitting down.'

Mum and Jessica hurried over. Mum looked concerned as she saw the way Sally was panting.

'You're right,' she said. 'She doesn't look right. Maybe I'd better take her temperature.' She fetched the thermometer from the pet first-aid kit and checked. 'It's slightly raised, but not much,' she said. 'Jessica, can you get her some water?'

Jessica fetched the water. Sally licked a little and stood and panted some more.

'Do you think you should take her to the vet's?' Jessica asked.

'Surgery will be shut for the evening,' Mum said. 'And you're only supposed to ring them after hours if it's a real emergency. I'll wait ten minutes and see how she is. If she's no better I'll give the vet a ring then.' She unclipped Sally's lead. 'Come on, girl, come inside.'

Sally went through to the playroom and, after moving round and round, finally found a comfy position under the table and lay down.

We watched her anxiously. To our relief, her breathing started to slow down and she looked slightly less distressed.

'She seems a bit better,' Mum said. 'I'll leave her a little longer while I fix supper.'

As Mum put a pan of water on to boil, Jessica started getting cutlery out to lay the table. I sat down, a wave of tiredness overwhelming me.

Jessica gave me a pointed look. 'You could help.'

I glared at her, fed up with her nagging. 'I'm tired.'

'Yeah, hanging round on a film set must be so exhausting,' Jessica replied witheringly.

'Leave Sophie alone, Jessica,' Mum said, going though to the playroom to check on Sally.

Jessica immediately turned on me. 'How can you be so mean?' she hissed. 'You can see what a day Mum's had and you won't even lift a finger to help.'

'I was just about to,' I protested.

'Yeah, right!' Jessica said, still keeping her voice low so Mum couldn't hear. 'I suppose you think now you're in a film you're too grand to do things like help out any more.' She slammed a knife down on the table. 'Well, it's not all about you, you, you. The rest of us do count too! You can be so selfish at times, Sophie! You really can!'

And with that she turned and ran out of the kitchen.

✦

Chapter Nineteen

I stared after her furiously. How dare she say I was self-ish! A wave of hurt swept away my anger. It just wasn't true. Tears prickled my eyes. I wasn't being selfish and film-starry. Was I?

'Sally's looking a bit better,' Mum said, coming back into the kitchen. 'Where's Jessica?' she asked in surprise.

'She's just gone upstairs,' I said, quickly blinking back the tears. I looked at the door. 'I'm just going to get something,' I mumbled, and I hurried out of the kitchen.

I had to sort this out. Not knowing quite what I was going to do, I went up the stairs. Reaching Jessica's bedroom, I went to knock and then hesitated. What if she just shouted at me again? Suddenly I heard the sound of crying. Concern for Jess pushed everything else out of my mind.

'Jess?' I said, knocking on the door. 'Can I come in?'

There was a pause and then Jessica said something that sounded like yes.

I opened the door. She was sitting on her bed, her face wet with tears.

'What is it?' I said, quickly shutting the door behind me. 'Jess, what's wrong?'

'Oh, Sophie, I'm sorry,' she sobbed.

'It's OK,' I said.

'I've been a complete cow.' She sniffed. 'I've just been so upset about Dan. I've been taking it out on you. I shouldn't have.'

I sat down beside her. 'Why . . . why are you upset about Dan? I thought you were back together.'

'We are. It's just not working out. He can't seem to trust me.' She swallowed. 'I thought I'd say I was sorry and that would be that, but what happened is always there. It's like this big barrier between us.' She swallowed. 'I want it all to be just like it was, but I don't think it ever will be. I think I've messed things up for good.'

I didn't know what to say.

A tear trickled down Jessica's cheek. She brushed it away. 'But I shouldn't have taken it out on you. I'm really, really sorry. I've just been so stressed out and tense.'

'It doesn't matter,' I said. With a burst of honesty I added, 'I guess I might have been a bit selfish. I didn't mean to be, but I've just been so busy and there's been all this stuff going on.'

'What stuff?' Jessica asked. 'Ally and Harriet?'

I nodded. 'And Issy.' I told Jessica about Issy getting the part in the TV series and suddenly being friends with Georgina. 'I thought we were best friends, but now, now I don't know.' I looked at Jess. Her eyes were sympathetic and suddenly I found myself confessing my worst fear. 'What if I don't have any friends when the film finishes?'

'You will,' she said. 'Just make up with Ally and Harriet.'

'I tried,' I said. 'I saw them today when I got back from filming, but they wouldn't even speak to me.'

'Try again,' Jess said. 'You've always been such good friends. Whatever you argued about, you can make it up if you really want to. Just keep trying.' She managed a small smile. 'That's what you told me when Dan and I split up.'

I risked a small joke. 'And look where *you* ended up.'

Our eyes met and we grinned.

'I mean it, Sophie,' she said. 'You've got to make up with them. It's not worth losing an old friendship over a new one. Believe me, I know.'

My insides curled up at the thought of trying to speak to Ally and Harriet, but I knew, deep down, that Jessica was right. I *had* to make friends with them again. It was going to be hard, but I had to keep trying.

'What about you and Dan?' I said softly. 'What are you going to do?'

'Finish with him, I guess,' Jessica said. 'We can't go out if he won't trust me.'

'Maybe you should try talking to him again first,' I said. 'It might help.'

'It might,' she said, but it was obvious from the tone of her voice that she didn't really believe it.

There was a knock on Jessica's door.

'Are you OK in there?' Mum asked, and it was easy to hear the concern in her voice.

'We're fine,' we both said quickly before she could come in.

I turned to Jessica. 'I'll go,' I said in a low voice. I knew she wouldn't want Mum to see that she'd been crying.

She looked at me gratefully. 'Thanks.' As I stood up, she smiled. 'You know, you're not bad for a little sister.'

'You make an OK big sister too,' I said.

We smiled at each other and then I went downstairs, closing the door after me.

Mum was back in the kitchen. 'Everything all right?' she asked casually as I went in.

I could tell she knew that something had been going on. 'It's fine,' I said. 'Mum?' I hesitated. 'Can I go round to see Harriet and Ally?'

Mum turned and then smiled. 'Of course,' she said.

'Sophie.' Harriet stared at me.

I stood uncomfortably on the doorstep. 'Hi.'

For a moment neither of us said anything.

'Can . . . can we talk?' I said at last.

I had decided to try and make up with Harriet first. I had a feeling that she would be quicker to forgive me than Ally would. She hesitated. I looked at her beseechingly.

'Please?'

Harriet nodded. 'OK.'

Relief whooshed through me, but it was quickly squashed when she said, 'Ally's here. She's in my room.'

'Oh.'

Suddenly I wanted to turn and run. What would Ally say when she saw me? I swallowed. It didn't matter. I had to make up with both of them.

'Shall I get her?' Harriet asked, looking uncertainly towards the staircase.

I started to nod, but then the words just seemed to burst out of me. 'Oh, Harriet, I'm sorry!' I stepped quickly towards her. 'I don't want to argue any more. Please can we be friends again? I miss you.'

Harriet looked startled, but then her hazel eyes seemed to soften. 'I miss you too, Soph. I . . .'

'Harriet, what . . . *Sophie!*' I looked up. Ally had obviously come to se what Harriet was doing. She stared at me angrily from the staircase. 'What are *you* doing here?' she demanded.

For a moment I wanted to turn and run all the way

home, but then I saw that in her eyes, beside the anger, there was also unhappiness and hurt. Without thinking any more, I let all the things I'd been wanting to say rush out of me. 'I want to be friends. I'm sorry, I really am. I never meant to be nasty. I was just feeling hurt.' I searched Ally's face, desperate to make her understand. 'Don't you see? You'd arranged to go to Alton Towers without me – you hadn't even told me you were going! It felt like you didn't need me any more, like I didn't matter, and I hated it, so when Issy laughed I joined in. I know I shouldn't have and I didn't mean it, really I didn't. I'm sorry. I . . .' I looked from Ally to Harriet. 'Please – I don't want to argue any more.'

There was a silence. Ally and Harriet stared at me. I felt a hot blush rising in my cheeks. I swallowed. This wasn't how it was supposed to be. Wasn't now the moment when they were supposed to tell me it was all OK? No one spoke. Unable to bear the silence any longer and feeling like a complete idiot, I turned to go.

'Sophie!' Harriet burst out. She grabbed my arm. 'Don't go. I . . . I don't want to argue either. I want to be friends again.' She looked at Ally. 'We *both* do.'

My eyes flew to Ally's. She hesitated and then nodded. 'Harriet's right,' she said.

She half ran down the stairs and the next second we were all hugging. My eyes filled with tears, but this time they were happy tears.

'I hated you not being friends with me,' I said, sniffing.

'It's been horrible,' Harriet agreed.

'Really weird,' Ally said.

'Did you really feel left out?' Harriet asked me.

'Yeah,' I answered. 'The two of you were doing all this stuff without me. It was horrible.'

'But we felt left out of what you were doing. You had the filming,' Ally said. 'You were always talking about it. It sounded so cool and exciting, and you had all these new friends and you stopped ringing us.'

She looked at Harriet, who nodded.

'It was like you didn't need us any more,' Harriet said.

'But I'll always need you,' I protested. 'You're my best friends.'

'What about Issy?' Ally said.

There was a tense pause.

'She *is* my friend,' I said slowly. 'I like her. She can be fun.' I looked at their familiar faces. 'But she's not you.'

Ally grinned and linked her arm through mine. 'We're the best.'

I grinned back, feeling a wave of pure happiness. 'The very best!'

'And we're never going to argue again,' Harriet put in.

'Not ever,' I declared.

'I think we should have a sleepover to celebrate,' Ally said.

'I can't tonight – I'm filming tomorrow,' I said. 'But what about on Monday? That's my last day on the set.'

'OK,' Ally said.

'Come on. Let's go to my room,' Harriet said.

We started up the stairs.

'So how was Alton Towers?' I asked.

'Not as much fun as if you'd been there,' Harriet replied.

'But best of all, Mum says I can go there for my birthday in October,' Ally said. 'So we can all go together then. It'll be great.'

I smiled at them happily. 'Brilliant!' I said.

By the time I went home I was feeling so happy that I could have skipped down the road. Ally, Harriet and I were friends again. Suddenly life seemed a whole lot better. I wasn't going to have to go to secondary school on my own. In fact, it might even be quite fun.

I hurried through the gate and up the path. I couldn't wait to tell Mum that Ally, Harriet and I were friends again. But as I opened the back door the smile fell from my face.

'What's happened?' I gasped.

My entire family were in the kitchen. The table had been shoved against the wall and Sally was lying on a bed of newspapers and old towels in the centre of the floor.

Mum and Jessica were kneeling beside her. Tom was filling a plastic bowl with hot water. Dad was on the phone, an anxious frown on his face as he scribbled down some notes. He motioned to me to be quiet.

'Well, if he can come as soon as possible,' he was saying. 'We are rather inexperienced in these matters.'

I hurried over to Mum. Sally was panting hard, her eyes were half closed, but as she saw me her tail gave a feeble thump.

'What's the matter with her?' I whispered.

Before I could answer, Dad put the phone down. 'The vet will be here when he can. He's out at a calving at the moment and the vet I spoke to can't leave the surgery. But he's given me some instructions.' Dad pushed his hand through his hair and took a deep breath. 'He said the most important thing is to keep calm.'

'It's OK, Sally,' Jessica said, stroking the dog's heaving sides. 'You're going to be all right.'

'Here's the water,' Tom said.

'What's going on?' I demanded loudly.

Everyone looked at me. 'Sally . . .' Mum took a deep breath. 'Sally's having puppies.'

'Puppies!' I gasped. A wave of pure relief washed over me. I'd been thinking that Sally was about to die or something. The relief changed to shock. 'Puppies,' I echoed. 'Oh, wow!' I looked at the sandy-coloured dog. 'She's having puppies.'

'We know,' Tom said with a grin. He handed me the

bowl of water. 'Here, take this. I'm going to find the book we've got on dog care. It might have something in it.'

'It's in my room on the bookshelf,' Jessica said.

Tom hurried off.

I looked at the bowl in my hands. 'What's this for?'

'For cleaning her up after she's had the puppies,' Mum said. 'Go and wash your hands and then you can make yourself useful.'

'We need scissors, kitchen roll, a cardboard box and lots of old towels,' Dad said, looking at his notes. 'If any of the puppies aren't breathing, we've got to rub them with towels until they do.'

He started to collect the things we needed, while I ran to the sink to wash my hands.

'So Sally isn't just fat.'

'No,' Mum said. 'And it's why she's been acting so strangely the last few days – when she was ripping up newspapers, she was trying to make a nest to have her puppies in.'

'Mum!' Jessica exclaimed. 'Quick! I think she's having one!'

Dad dropped the kitchen roll and we both hurried over. A ripple seemed to run down Sally's side.

'I've got the book!' Tom called, coming into the kitchen. 'It says the puppies will come out one by one, each in their own sac.' He stopped. 'Oh, wow!'

We all watched in amazed silence as a puppy was

born. Heaving herself round, Sally started to lick it all over, cleaning away the white sac. The puppy gave a squirm and a wriggle. His eyes were closed, his black fur was wet and his ears were slicked back against his head. He squeaked and began to move closer to Sally's tummy.

'What do we do?' I whispered, awed.

'Nothing,' Mum said softly. 'Just watch.'

'He's feeding,' Jessica breathed, as the pup buried his head in Sally's golden hair and started to suck. She glanced round at us. Her eyes shone with tears. 'Isn't it the most amazing thing you've ever seen?'

'Definitely,' I agreed, sniffing.

'Cool,' Tom said, nodding.

He sounded laid back, but I could tell from the way he cleared his throat as he watched the tiny puppy feeding that he was just as moved as Jessica and me.

Dad put his hand on Mum's shoulder. 'A new life,' he said, smiling at her.

Sally laid her head down and started to pant again.

'And it looks like there's another one coming,' Mum said.

When the vet arrived an hour and a half later, Sally was lying back on a clean set of towels, letting her four new puppies feed.

He checked her over. 'Seems that's all she's having,' he announced. 'Two boys and two girls. All healthy.'

We exchanged delighted looks.

'What I can't understand is why no one guessed she was pregnant,' Mum said. 'Surely the rescue kennels that Mrs Ling got her from would have noticed her condition.'

The vet nodded. 'But sometimes mistakes can be made. If there aren't many puppies, it can sometimes be hard to tell when a bitch is pregnant.' He smiled. 'Looks like her owner's going to be in for a shock. When does she get back?'

'Next week,' Mum said.

'You should be fine until then. Keep the puppies warm and the mum clean. If you've got any concerns give me a ring.'

'I will. Thank you,' Mum said.

Dad showed the vet out. As he came back into the kitchen, he breathed out in relief. 'I can't believe we got through it,' he said.

'Four healthy puppies,' Jessica agreed.

'And a healthy Sally,' I said.

'Result,' Tom said.

Mum smiled at the little puppies. 'Look at them. Aren't they sweet? Those little paws and noses.' She looked up, her eyes half teasing. 'Maybe I should become a dog-breeder as well as a pet-sitter.'

'No!' Dad, Tom, Jessica and I exclaimed, making Sally look round and wag her tail.

Mum grinned. 'You all sound very sure.'

'One new business is *quite* enough,' Dad said.

'And one litter of puppies is quite enough for me,' Tom said.

'Go on, you think they're sweet really,' Jessica teased him.

Tom raised his eyebrows.

'You do!' Jessica and I said together.

'OK, maybe they *are* quite cute,' Tom gave in.

Dad looked at us and smiled. 'This evening might have been a bit traumatic, but it's good to see you three getting on again.'

Tom, Jessica and I exchanged looks.

'It's been a difficult time recently, hasn't it?' Mum said softly.

For a moment none of us said anything. I thought about everything that had happened in the last few months – me doing the film, Mum's new business, Jessica and Dan, Tom and his band. Mum was right. It had been difficult.

'There's been a lot happening,' I said.

'A lot of changes,' Dad agreed. He put an arm round my shoulders and Jessica's. 'But we're pulling through.'

'Together,' Jessica said.

Mum smiled. 'Like a family should.'

✦

Chapter Twenty

'Will you sign my call sheet?'

'And mine please.'

It was Monday afternoon and Issy and I were finished on set. We were charging about the green room and the set getting as many people as possible to sign their names on our call sheets. It had been Issy's idea. Apparently she always did it at the end of each film or play she worked on.

'Alan!' Issy cried as Alan walked into the green room. 'Over here!'

I hurried after her. I definitely wanted to get Alan's autograph. I had been really pleased when I had found out he had been called in on the last day to shoot an extra bit of dialogue with me. I had wanted a chance to say goodbye.

'Can you sign my sheet too please?' I asked eagerly.

'Of course.' As Issy dashed off, he took my sheet, wrote something and signed his name. 'There you are. And I mean it.'

I looked at what he had written:

Dearest Sophie, If I had a real daughter I'd like her to be just like you. From your 'Papa' — Alan Thomas

I blushed. 'Thank you,' I said.

He smiled. 'It's been a pleasure working with you. Maybe we'll work together again another time.'

'I'd really like that,' I said, and then suddenly I hugged him.

He kissed the top of my head. 'Take care, sweetheart.'

As Alan walked off, I felt a lump in my throat. I was really going to miss him and all the others — Laurence, Cathy, Steve, Jules, Gary, Margaret, Joan, Gillian . . .

I stopped, realizing I hadn't got Gillian's autograph yet. I knew she was on set because she had a scene to film that evening. Maybe she was in Make-up. I told Margaret where I was going and hurried over to see.

Gillian was there, reading a magazine while Jules arranged her hair. She looked up when I came in and smiled. 'All finished?'

I nodded. I felt suddenly shy. 'Will . . . will you sign my call sheet for me please, Gillian?' I asked.

'Of course.'

She took the sheet wrote something and signed it. 'So what are you doing next?' she asked me as she handed it back.

'Nothing at the moment,' I admitted. 'Just going to school.'

'Do you still want to do more acting and go to drama school?' Gillian asked.

'Yes!' I said.

She smiled. 'Then I'm sure you will. You're very talented.'

I blushed. 'Thank you.' I glanced at her. 'Thank you for everything,' I said hesitantly. 'You've been really nice.'

'It's my pleasure,' Gillian said. For a moment I wondered if she was going to hug me, like Alan had, but she just squeezed my hand. 'Good luck, Sophie. With whatever you do.' She smiled. 'Now off you go and get some more autographs.'

As I left the room, I read what she had written:

To Sophie, The bright lights are waiting for you. Follow them, but always stay true to yourself. With love and best wishes — Gillian

I swallowed. I knew I was going to miss Gillian almost more than anyone.

By the time Dad arrived to collect me I had about forty names on my sheet and there was hardly any room for Issy to fit her message. But she managed it.

To my bestest friend, Sophie, ring me EVERY day.
Lots and lots and lots of love from Issy xoxoxoxoxoxoxox

'I'm really going to miss you,' she wailed, hugging me as I read her message. 'Now you write on mine.'

I took her call sheet.

To Issy, I wrote. I hesitated. What should I put? I remembered a rhyme I had read once and quickly wrote it down:

A ring is round and has no end and that's how long I'll be your friend.
Lots of love, Sophie

'I love it!' Issy said, reading it. She hugged me. 'I promise I'll phone and e-mail you every day.'

I smiled but didn't say anything. I liked Issy, but I knew now that it was Ally and Harriet who really mattered. They were my best friends. Whatever I did, wherever I went, they would always be there for me, just like I would always be there for them.

'Come on, Sophie,' Dad called.

I gave Issy a last hug. 'Good luck with the TV series.'

'Thanks.' She smiled. 'And good luck with getting some more work soon.'

'I won't hold my breath,' I said.

'Sophie!' Dad called again.

'Coming! Bye, Is.'

'Bye, Soph,' she said, and that was it.

I turned and hurried across the car park to where Dad was waiting, my autographed call sheet in my hand.

As we drove out of the film lot, I took one last look at the huge factory-like building, the security fences, the parkland where outdoor scenes could be filmed, and then we were through the gates and away. Filming was over.

'Welcome home!'

As I opened the back door, a loud shout greeted me and I stopped in my tracks. The kitchen was full of people who were all looking at me and smiling. The table was packed with food and there were streamers hanging from the walls.

'Hi, darling,' Mum said, hurrying forward. 'We thought we'd have a little party to celebrate the end of filming.' She hugged me.

'Wow!' I said, looking round.

Ally and Harriet were standing by the window, grinning. Tom's band, without Zak, were standing around the crisps. Jessica was there with her friends Nicole and Laura, and our next-door neighbours were there too.

'Have a drink,' Jessica said, getting me a can of Coke out of the fridge.

I stepped forward and suddenly everyone was crowding round me and patting me on the back. Tom turned some music on.

'It's party time!' he said. 'Come on, everyone, through to the lounge!'

'Tom, turn it down!' Mum called as people started moving in that direction.

I reached Jessica and took the drink. 'I can't believe it,' I said, looking round at the party. 'Dad didn't say anything!'

'That's because it was supposed to be a surprise.' She looked at me. 'A good surprise?'

'A very good surprise,' I said. I glanced at her as I pulled the tab on my Coke. 'So, have you spoken to Dan yet?'

She looked down. 'Yeah,' she said, her voice suddenly so quiet that I had to move in close to hear her above the music and the chatting. 'He . . . he said that he felt things weren't working too and that he couldn't trust me. He agreed we should split up.'

'Oh, Jess,' I said.

She shrugged. 'I guess I knew that's what he would say.' She smiled bravely. 'But look, I'm not going to be sad. It's your party.'

Just then the back door opened. Jessica froze as Dan stopped in the doorway. Their eyes met across the crowd. For a long moment they looked at each other and then he half held out his hand. Jessica walked towards him as if in a daze. I watched as they went outside into the garden.

'Sophie!' Ally said, grabbing hold of me. 'Did you know about the party?'

'No, I didn't have a clue,' I said, dragging my eyes away from the back door. I wondered what Dan wanted.

'Your mum says you can still come round for a sleep-over tonight,' Harriet said.

'Come and have some Kettle Crisps,' Ally said, dragging me over to the table. 'And then can we go and see the puppies. They are *so* cute!'

The puppies! I remembered that Mum was supposed to have rung Mrs Ling to tell her the news. 'Mum!' I gasped, going into the lounge, where Mum was standing with Barbara, our next-door neighbour. 'What did Mrs Ling say?'

'She was astonished, but when she got over her shock she was delighted,' Mum said, her face breaking into a smile. 'She's such a nice lady. She said she's going to recommend Purr-fect for Pets to all her friends.'

I grinned. 'Another contented customer.'

Tom was standing nearby. He overheard and raised his can. 'To Purr-fect for Pets,' he said, 'the best pet-sitting business there is, and to Mum, the best Mum there is.'

'Thank you, Tom,' Mum said, smiling.

Tom looked at me. 'And to Sophie,' he said, 'our film star.'

Everyone raised their glasses. 'To Purr-fect for Pets, Annie and Sophie,' they said.

Hearing the back door open, I glanced round and saw Jessica and Dan coming in from outside. I stared. They were holding hands!

Jessica grinned at me.

My heart felt like it was about to burst with delight. Filming might be over, but suddenly I didn't care. My life was great just the way it was. I had my friends and my family and everyone was happy.

Just then the phone rang.

'Sophie! It's for you,' Mum called.

I fought my way to the phone.

'Sophie?'

It was a woman's voice. Who was it?

'Sophie, it's Sheila Blake here.'

Sheila Blake! Of course! The casting director!

Sheila laughed. 'You sound like your having a bit of a party.'

'We arc,' I said.

I moved through the lounge and into the dining room, where it was quieter. Why was Sheila ringing? What did she want?

'Well, I won't keep you long,' Sheila said. 'I'm just ringing to find out whether you would be interested in auditioning for a play I'm casting.'

'A play!' I exclaimed in delight. 'Yes, yes, of course I'd be interested.'

'It's being performed over Christmas and New Year at the Palace Theatre in Nottingham,' Sheila said.

My thoughts whirled. I could be in a play at a really big theatre! Wow!

'What play is it?' I asked her eagerly.

'*The Lion, the Witch and the Wardrobe*,' Sheila replied. 'I'd like you to audition for the role of Lucy.'

'Lucy!' I exclaimed, my voice sounding like a mouse being strangled in mid-squeak. 'You want *me* to audition for Lucy?'

'Only if you want to,' Sheila said.

Want to? I gaped. I pictured myself on an enormous stage with rows and rows of people watching me as I knelt beside a great fallen lion. I gaped some more.

Unfortunately Sheila seemed to take my stunned silence for uncertainty. 'Well, you don't have to make up your mind right now, Sophie. Have a think about it for a few hours if you like.'

Luckily my brain and mouth managed to get it together. 'No,' I gabbled. 'I don't need to think. I want to do it – I really do.'

'Well, go and get your mum, then, and I'll have a chat to her about the auditions,' Sheila said, a smile in her voice.

I ran to get Mum, who was now in the kitchen. 'Sheila wants to talk to you!' I gasped. 'About an audition! It's for a play!'

'An audition?' Mum handed me the plate of sausage

rolls she was carrying. 'Here, take these. I'll go and speak to her.'

I flew back to the party with the sausage rolls. Just wait till everyone heard my news!

I pushed the door open. Tom was teasing Ally and Harriet. Nick and Raj had let Baxter and Wilson in and were feeding them crisps. Jess and Dan were standing by the window, talking softly, and Dad — Dad was walking towards me, a smile on his face.

'Ah, sausage rolls,' he said. 'My favourite.' He popped one into his mouth and put an arm round my shoulder. 'Having a good time, sweetheart?' he asked and, looking up at him, I saw that his eyes were full of love.

All of a sudden, my news about the audition didn't seem to matter quite so much. I looked around the room. Yes, I wanted to be Lucy — I really did. But it was just one play. There would be other plays and other films. It was my family and friends who were really important.

I thought about Dad's question. *Am I having a good time?*

'Yes,' I said, hugging him happily. 'I am. I really am.'

★